From forty feet, there was no way he could miss. Taking his breath in, he let his body mold to the earth. The rifle settled and the trigger slack was taken up. He fired twice. The suppressor didn't completely kill sound, but it distributed it and made it harder to hear and identify. From a hundred or so meters one would hear little if anything, and then it would be indistinct. It could have been no more than a big bird farting.

The back of the Russian's head separated. Only his legs trembling in death spasm made any movement. He was brain dead. That's one.

Look for all these TOR books by Barry Sadler

BARRY SADLER

Author of PHÚ NHÂM and THE SHOOTER

SOMETIMES TERRORISTS STRIKE
TOO CLOSE TO HOME

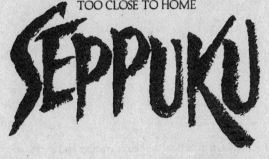

SEPPUKU

TOR

A TOM DOHERTY ASSOCIATES BOOK

This is a work of fiction. All the characters and events portrayed in this book are fictional, and any resemblance to real people or incidents is purely coincidental.

SEPPUKU

First printing: February 1988

A TOR Book

Published by Tom Doherty Associates, Inc.
49 West 24th Street
New York, NY 10010

ISBN: 0-812-58845-2
Can. No.: 0-812-58846-0

Printed in the United States of America

0 9 8 7 6 5 4 3 2 1

SEPPUKU

ONE

THEY HAD TO MOVE THE COPILOT OUT OF HIS SEAT. IT wasn't easy; dead meat doesn't move by itself. The man in the stocking mask tried to avoid the brain matter which had splattered all over the instrument panel. He'd have one of the stewardesses clean up the mess later, but not too much later. In this heat it would soon begin to deteriorate and decay. Already the cloying, acid-sweet copper smell was hanging ripe and thick in the still air. A hand pushed him out of the way.

"Let me do it."

The voice was strangely accented, the English not at all like the others of his race who spoke the Ferengi tongue. But then he was not like the others who had the blood and the words of the Prophet, blessed be His name, to guide them.

He was Japanese. A most strange cool man with brain-fevered eyes who seldom spoke, but when he did you knew it was wise to listen: if not for the words of wisdom, then for your health. This one would kill instantly, without hesitation. And he was not afraid to die. Perhaps he was even anxious to. With such a one what could you do to frighten or discipline him?

He was the one who had made the example of the first hostage when their demands for the release of seven brothers from the hands of the West German police had not been agreed to. The Germans had been given until 1100 hours Berlin time to release their prisoners and put them on a plane to Damascus. At 1101 the Japanese had walked into the cockpit and, without a word, placed his .45 Colt automatic pistol to the back of the copilot's head and blown the brains out.

Now the body would be tossed out on the tarmac. The Germans and the world would know they were serious about their promises, and Hasan had no doubt that the Japanese would not hesitate to do exactly as he had threatened.

Now the Germans had five hours, then he would kill ten of the passengers. After that the Germans would be granted five more hours. When that time passed there would be nothing left to negotiate with; all would be dead. He would kill the rest of the passengers and then detonate the explosive charges they had set and destroy the aircraft and themselves with it. He would do exactly as he had said he would.

Ahh, by the Prophet, blessed be His name, it was very difficult to rationalize with fanatics.

He, Hasan Salmeh, was of course ready to die, following the orders of his masters and leaders. Still, it was not such an unpleasant existence that he was overly anxious to gain the pleasures of paradise. As for the other three, ibn-Karim, Yousef Safar, and Mustafa al-Hakim, they would also follow the path laid down for them by their Imam. If it was necessary, they would die; but like Hasan they were different from this small strange man who had come to them from the Japanese Red Army. It would not be with pleasure that they would give this life so soon when the oldest of them was not yet thirty years of age.

Yoshi Tomanaga, with Hasan at his side, dragged the body out of the cockpit. The Colt Combat Commander .45 pistol, a gift to him from the leader of his cell in Tokyo, was ready in the event that any of the passengers panicked or did something foolish.

As they entered the passenger section, a groan began to rise into a wail as the female passengers saw the body of the copilot. It was stopped instantly by a harsh command from ibn-Karim. The threatened cries and screams were instantly reduced to mere muffled groans as the women passengers buried their faces in their hands, fighting to choke back the growing swell of vomit and fear which rose up into the backs of their throats.

The men, most of them, tried to look stoically on, but the fear was with them too, especially those who were Jewish or American. They knew that if there was more killing to be done they would be the first to go.

The hatch was already open to permit a bit of fresh air to enter the aircraft where the temperature seemed close to that of a blast furnace. The terrorists would have preferred to keep it closed, but the air conditioning was not sufficient to fight off the heat of the midday desert. If they had not opened it, the passengers and they themselves would have soon been overcome by the heat, which even now was rising in waves off the tarmac, dancing and shimmering.

It was into this heat that Yoshi tossed the remains of the copilot. The sound of his body hitting dully on the tarmac was heard, or imagined to be heard, all the way to the rear of the aircraft.

Across the field, on the roof of the terminal, John Freeman prayed that he had the right settings on his camera and that the telephoto lens had been able to penetrate the shadow of the aircraft doorway enough to bring out the faces of the men who had thrown the body out. If so, he'd have his pay for the next two months. So far, no one had a picture worth a shit of any of the terrorists. This one shot would be worth ten grand to any of the networks. He'd know within the hour, after he processed the black-and-white roll in his hotel room. The dead man was already forgotten. He'd seen worse.

The radio, which was kept open, began to crackle and sputter seconds after the body hit the ground. Yoshi had no real interest in what was said; he left that to Karim, the leader of the fighters from the Black September. All he knew, all he had to know, was whether the Germans had agreed to their demands or not. That was all he would accept; there would be no negotiations. No extension of deadlines, even if the Palestinians with him wanted one. Any attempt to change any of his orders and he would kill them, too, and then push the button of the remote-control detonator in his shirt pocket, destroying everyone.

Even in death one could be victorious. It was simple, it was clean. As Musashi said in his *Book of Five Rings*, either one was victorious or he died. There were no other options. These Palestinians thought he was there to do their bidding in this thing. Fools! He was there for his own purposes. The plight of the Palestinians meant less than nothing to him, except for the value he chose to put on them. This thing was being done for himself, not for any other reason. He felt that Karim, who seemed to be slightly more intelligent than his companions, understood, which was good. He did not like childish attempts at subterfuge.

The voice of the German consul was frantic over the crackle of the radio, pleading for more time in which to meet their demands, begging them to release their hostages, or at least the women and children.

Karim felt Yoshi's eyes on the nape of his neck. The hairs stood up, his mouth felt dry. He wanted to accept a lesser deal to negotiate. But if he did, he would have to kill Yoshi and he was not sure he would be able to. The Japanese was never off guard, though he appeared relaxed, even tranquil. Karim's instincts told him absolutely that Yoshi was the better of them. He cursed himself for the earlier decision to let their comrade from the JRA, the Japanese Red Army, take charge of the detonator. A fly landed on the corner of his mouth; absently he brushed the insect away and spoke into the radio's handset.

"You have our demands. There are no other conditions acceptable. You have five hours. We will open the radio again in four hours. If your government has followed our demands and we have confirmation that our comrades in the struggle against Zionist oppression are free, then we will have something to discuss. If not, then more will die. You have seen the evidence of our sincerity. All other deaths will be the responsibility of the German government, not ours. Their lives are in your hands!"

Clicking off the radio, he felt relieved that he had managed to speak firmly, without a quaver in his voice. Behind him he could feel the slight tension in Yoshi's body relax. The hairs on his neck went down.

Time dragged as slowly as thick blood. Each second ticking away took hours. Twice the hostages were permitted to take water. Only one at a time, and under guard, were they permitted to use the toilets, and the doors were kept open at all times. Even the women had to perform their bodily functions in plain sight.

In his mind, Yoshi knew nearly all who would be taken next. Sitting in the first-class section, which had been cleared out, he went over the passports of all the passengers.

Once his mind was clear about them he went back into the passenger section and began to identify them, letting his eyes rest on one and then another, trying to sense which, if any, would give him any problems. There was one, an American with press credentials, who looked at him steadily, directly in the eyes. Calm, clear, brown eyes. Yoshi felt there was a calmness to this one. He was not afraid in the way the other passengers were. If any would fight or cause a problem, it would be him. Yoshi felt a kindred spirit in him, and knew that just the look in the reporter's eyes had condemned him to death. Care must be taken with this one. He looked again at the blue-covered American passport: Abrams. A Jewish name.

He did not understand the Palestinians' racial hatred of Jews. From what he knew they were both from the same roots, with many similar customs and practices. But it was not his concern.

One hour and fifteen minutes until the radio line opened again at 1600 hours. He went down both sides of the aisle, his eyes touching one, then another. In some he could feel the fear; they knew they had been selected for something and they hoped it was not what they knew it was going to be. They deluded themselves with other thoughts, that perhaps they were to be released as a gesture. Yes, perhaps that was why the Oriental with the almost priestlike air had looked at them.

There were others he looked at also: women traveling with their children; two boys, about ten and twelve, traveling alone to join their father who worked on drilling rigs in the Negev. He almost smiled at them, but this was not the time. His selections made, he returned to the first-class section, ignoring the eyes following his every movement.

Accidentally, he brushed against the arm of one of the stewardesses, a petite brunette with features of Mediterranean cast. He bowed slightly. *"Gomen nasai."* An apology. Because one held power over others was not any reason to behave in a rude manner. Indeed, that was the time when one should be most considerate and mannerly, for it was a noble thing to do. It was samurai.

His associates did not understand this. He could feel them swell with power as they took control of the aircraft, its passengers and crew. And with each passing minute, as the fear among the hostages increased, so did their own feelings of self-importance. They were small men with no real merit in their spirits. They had bad karma to them. He did not much like them.

TWO

YOSHI TOMANAGA CHECKED HIS SEIKO WATCH. THE time had passed again. Most regretful. Now he must get ready for the next event. He nodded to Hasan. They began to separate the selected ones from the other passengers. One at a time they were taken back to the station by the galley.

The beginning of a protest from one of the male passengers was quickly silenced by a strike across the face from a pistol, fracturing the cheekbone. This one was then taken in place of the next name on the list. He never knew that his actions had given another a chance to live a bit longer.

As they were brought into the galley area, their hands were tied behind them. Five and five. That would make the Germans take notice. What was there in the Western mind about killing women? Did they not have, after all, equal rights?

The first to be brought up was the American with the calm eyes. His hands, fingers laced, were placed behind his neck. Two men escorted him, one behind, his left hand holding the collar of Abrams' suit coat, the pistol hand held close to his right side in the event that their hostage tried to make a circling move and counterattack. The man in front walked crabwise, his pistol also held a safe distance from Abrams' reach.

The passengers knew nothing of the terrorists' demands, or the timetable set for their deaths, but when the third person, a middle-aged hausfrau from Bonn, was half dragged as she cried hysterically, the sour smell of fear was immediate and real.

Once the ten were isolated, Yoshi took over. This was his job, to do it clean, without mistakes. To have to shoot someone twice would be very bad form. He did not trust his emotional comrades to do things properly.

He checked his watch again; it was important to be punctual. As the Americans said, time was money and, perhaps more important in this case, it was life.

Pushing Abrams to the front, Yoshi did not use excessive force or violence in his actions. He knew it would not be needed. This one had accepted his finality. That was good. It might make the rest of the job easier. He knew it would become unpleasant as the captives reacted to their impending demise. He hoped that the American Jew would set an example which the rest of them might emulate.

The glare of daylight through the open door was harsh. The light breeze which ran across the tarmac was hotter than the ambient air temperature, but it was still refreshing as it evaporated the sweat retained in clothing, causing for a brief moment the illusion of being cooled.

Jeremiah Abrams had no illusions of any kind about what his fate was to be. He was going to die. He had looked the Oriental in the eyes earlier and saw his death and knew why. In a way he was almost flattered. If there had been anything he could have attempted which might have saved the hostages, he would have tried. But any effort on his part would most likely have led to the random slaughter of others in the enclosed environment of the aircraft. They had him and that was that.

The light hurt his eyes as he stepped out onto the platform, guided by the somehow comforting hand of the Japanese. He was glad this man was going to do the job. Abrams felt no hate in him. He was not the same as the Palestinians; He was calmer, gentler, and, Abrams knew, infinitely more dangerous. But he was not a sadist. He would do what had to be done as quickly and cleanly as possible.

There was a wonder to it all. Reality in this

time frame was somehow distant, unreal. He
had known from the time they had taken over
the aircraft that he was not going to come out
of it. Now there was no hate left in him. There
had never been any true hate in him for anyone
or anything.

He was going to die and all that was left was
a strange, not unpleasant, detached curiosity
to find out finally what lay at the end of the
road. Were the great religions, any of them,
correct? Was there anything more? The last
great secret was about to be opened to him. He
wished the Oriental would get on with it.

The bullet took him at the small hollow at
the base of the skull, angling upward into the
brain, exiting over his left eye. There was no
pain. For a ten-thousandth of a second his mind
registered a bright light. The face of God or the
entrance to nothing?

For Yoshi the unpleasant part began. Still, he
was pleased and even envious of the manner in
which Abrams had gone to his destiny. It was
good. He had died well. But the others . . . The
men weren't too bad. They trembled, some had
tears and tried to yell farewells to family still in
the plane. And one, to Yoshi's infinite disgust,
loosed his bowels and bladder. The stench was
incredible. But most went quietly enough.

It was the women who upset him most.
Three had died well, but two of them attempted to break away and run. It required

more than one shot each to silence their screaming as their bodies rolled down the stairs to join the others on the runway.

The woman from Bonn had been stronger than she looked. When they led her to the ramp, she had twisted and kicked away from them, screaming obscenities. Yoshi felt very bad about that. It took two shots in her head to stop her and it was very messy.

All this he knew was being recorded by cameras in the terminal and he had no doubt that the brothers held in Germany would now have a much better chance of being released. The Western world did not know how to react to absolute and pure violence.

There had not been and there would not be any negotiation. He would not permit them to fall into the trap of letting the enemy buy time at their expense. What was to be done had to be accomplished quickly. Time was their enemy. There was always the unexpected, the un-planned-for thing which could occur if they waited.

No, he would make them go by his time schedule, and if they did not, then he would without hesitation kill everyone in the aircraft, including himself. That would make them pay attention when the next group of hostages was taken. Not that that really mattered to him.

For Yoshi it didn't matter, as long as he was true to himself. Death was nothing; only the

manner of it mattered. That would always be of
his own choosing. He was certain of that.
When his time came he would be the master of
his karma. Death would be by his choice.

Ah, that was good. When fear of the great
black was no longer a factor in one's life, then
and only then was one truly a spirit free to walk
as did the samurai of old: as gods among the
lesser animals of the earth.

As for Hasan and his "brothers," they were,
though they did not show it, relieved when
Yoshi took over the job of executioner. None of
them had ever shot a person in cold blood, and
none had ever killed a woman.

After the executions, the Germans believed
them. So did the rest of the world after the
pictures were shown on television. Unfortunately, the distance was such that the face of
the executioner could not be clearly seen,
though it was obvious he was Oriental.

All the intelligence agencies arrived at the
same conclusion: He had to be a member of
the JRA, the same group who had participated
in the Lod Airport massacre. That fact made
everyone more nervous, certain that there
could be no negotiations or dialogue with the
terrorists. They would do exactly as they had
threatened and kill *everyone* on board the
aircraft.

Public outcry reached a crescendo in a matter of hours, as embassies and consulates were swamped with calls and telegrams demanding they release the prisoners in Germany in exchange for the lives of the passengers.

It would be done, though there would be much gnashing of teeth and tearing of hair over it from the security agencies. Once more, convicted terrorists would be set free to continue their bloody work. Once again, the great nations of the world would be held helpless before the demands of a few fanatics.

The frustration was incredible. Something had to be done. Sooner or later the terrorists would go too far and then maybe the world would support real countermeasures. Until then, however . . .

In Arlington, Virginia, the executive officer of the Delta Force went over the list of passenger names. He had been in Vietnam with one of the names on the list. His heart skipped a beat, then picked up a slightly faster pace. It had jumped off the list at him. Perhaps this was it. Maybe, just maybe, the Palestinians had finally broken the camel's back.

Suddenly the day was not nearly so dismal. There was a ray of light breaking through the overcast as he checked his Rolodex, found the number he wanted, and made a call to the Hill, chuckling to himself at the manner in which God works His many wonders.

He was humming an old song about happy days when a voice came on the other end of the line.

"Good morning, Senator Manchester's office. May we help you?"

It was a bright, young voice, eager and helpful. It did him good to dampen her spirits a bit. Working for Manchester, she was probably a leftover fucking hippie.

"Right, this is a priority call. Put the senator on the line and tell him to use his fucking scrambler."

THREE

"I WANT THEM, DO YOU HEAR ME, AND I AM NOT THE only one. This time the motherfuckers are going to pay in the coin they understand best. I want them dead, and I want them that way soon!"

Ex-Special Forces officer and now publisher of a popular line of men's adventure magazines, Green knew exactly what his visitor meant. He had been preaching the same thing since '68. But it was a surprise to hear it from this man.

"Calm down, Jerry, and give me a readout. This is a radical change and if I'm going to help, which I want to do, I have to have the full story of why this sudden change of heart and how it came about."

His face red with passion and fifty years of good brandy, Gerald R. Manchester did as he was asked with difficulty. Settling his heavy, well-dressed, and well-fleshed frame into the uncomfortable chair Green kept in front of his desk, he wiped his brow to rid it of the perspiration which had built up during the passion of his declarations. He was one of those who had perspiration, not sweat.

"This time they've gone too far. They have stuck their noses in the shit and now some very influential people want them cut off, literally cut off, do you hear me?" His voice started to rise again but was brought back to normal by the calm lowering motion of Green's hand.

"All right, tell me who wants them and why this time and not the others?"

Manchester sucked in a breath, still struggling to gain control of his emotions. He gave himself a moment, letting his eyes wander around the office, the walls lined with plaques and awards from a dozen foreign countries for services rendered by Green and his staff, almost all of whom were ex-veterans. "The April twelfth incident in Libya."

Green nodded his head. "I haven't had the readout on it yet; you know I just got back in from Bangkok." Normally, he would have had almost as much data as the CIA did; he kept on top of all major and most minor international terrorist activities.

"Well, the sons of bitches didn't do their homework. The copilot they shot was the nephew of a Member of Parliament, and an influential one. On top of that, one of the Americans, a journalist, was butchered by them. His head was literally blown off his shoulders.

"His name, if you haven't read the papers yet, was Abrams, Jeremiah Abrams." Manchester waited expectantly and wiped his face again.

Green blanched slightly as the name sunk in. The only other sign of being bothered was when he replaced the pinch of tobacco in his jaw, spitting the old cud into a plastic-foam cup kept close at hand for that purpose.

So that was it. Jeremiah Abrams. That pulled a lot of loose strings together. Medal of Honor recipient, Jewish, a conscientious objector who'd gone to Nam as a medic and been one of the last to be decorated. Influential family. The darling of the Jewish War Veterans of America, a man who had later become a close personal friend of the President and had campaigned for him, helping to pull in the Jewish vote.

Besides which he was, one of the most gentle and truly courageous people Green had ever met. Now he'd been butchered and you could bet your ass that there were people from more than one sector calling for vengeance.

He had also been Manchester's son-in-law.

Restraining himself, he spat a brown glob into the cup. "Anything else?"

Manchester rose, walking heavily over to the wall, staring at but not seeing the inscription on the plaque from the Army of El Salvador, thanking Green and his men for their assistance in the past.

"Of course there's more. Much more. Others were killed, men and women with influential friends and families. One of them was the brother of Anton Villon, the French Minister of Culture. If you're not familiar with the name it's because he is an artist and sculptor from Paris. Looks Jewish but isn't. To lots of people he is the greatest thing to happen to the French art world since Matisse. He is, to say the least, very, very popular there. Anyway, it appears the terrorists did not have enough Americans and Jews to make up their ten, so they just picked one other more or less at random and they killed Henri Villon.

"For that, we now even have the French finally pissed off enough to at least give what information they have on the terrorists. No matter; they couldn't have picked a worse time. For the first time several governments are in agreement about what to do. Those butchers have to be punished!"

"That's something of a major change of thinking for you, isn't it, Jerry? We've been on opposite sides of the fence most of our lives. You have never supported armed force being used in any circumstances. And I know that you didn't approve of your daughter marrying a Jew. So why the change now? And why have you come to me?"

Manchester whipped around. The hollows under his eyes seemed suddenly much deeper, the words heavier, weary. "It's true, I didn't want Angela to marry him. My family have been staunch Catholics for generations. But that doesn't mean that I didn't like the boy and respect him. He was a good man and one of the few who proved to the world that you don't have to be a killer to be a hero.

"We needed him in this world. There were plans for his future that might have made this miserable globe a tiny bit better place to live in. Now he's gone and what happened to him was not an act of war or an effort to liberate oppressed peoples, but the actions of criminals, psychotic maniacs. And as such they must be caught and punishment made in language they understand!

"As for why you, that's obvious. I know you have supplied information, and even samples of equipment, to the CIA and military. Over the years, you've built your own sources of information and are probably number one on the list of what you call the good-old-boy network. And more important, for over twenty years we have, as you said, been on opposite sides of the fence. But you have never lied to me and in spite of our differences we have been, I think, friends."

Green stood up and walked to the window where he could look out at the snowcaps of the Rockies. "Who else is in the game and what kind of support can we look for?"

Manchester moved to stand beside him, his chest heaving as though he'd been climbing stairs. The effort to control himself and the conflict going on within his conscience was obvious.

"You will have support. You know that because of policy and international diplomacy the terrorists have time and again gotten away with things like this. Well, the political climate has not changed. But the mood has. You can look for full support as to information and intelligence and even to weapons and documents if required. The British SIS, and through them the Canadians, are with us on this and you will have the support of the American intelligence community as well. And money is not an object. Your people can just about name their price if they are successful."

Green nodded. "What about the Mossad? Will they help us as well?"

Manchester nodded his head wearily. "Yes, of course. This is more to their advantage than anyone else's." He did not like the Mossad and their past habits of violent retribution, an eye for an eye and all that kind of thing. They had, time and again, made sensitive situations in the Middle East more difficult for him. In his mind they were little better, if any, than the people they went after. And they had made one or two very bad blunders in the past. "That's all I can say for now. Are you in or are you out?"

Green turned around and spit into his cup with a vengeance. "You bet your ass I'm in. I've been waiting since '68 for someone to finally do something. Not that they'll follow through with it; they never do. But at least it's a start.

"Now, give me the rest of it. Don't hold out on me, because the men I have in mind to do this job are going to know everything about you, and if anything fucks up they'll come looking for you. So, no politician double talk, no bullshit. You give me everything you have or take it elsewhere and I'll forget we ever had this talk."

It was done. Manchester had finally committed himself and it seemed as if a great weight had been taken from him. He was able to turn some of his guilt for the programs he had supported in the past over to another. It helped to ease the burden of conscience.

Deliberate, calculated death and terror had touched him and it frightened him. As a senior United States senator he had many times in the past voted and fought against appropriations for such projects as the Delta Force and special counterterrorist teams with international strike capabilities, believing sincerely that violence only begat more violence.

He had thought the current wave of such acts would wither and die as the organizations involved—the PLFP, al-Fatah, Tupamaros, and the rest—became more sophisticated. They would surely become aware that their activities were doing them more harm in the world's eyes than good. But it hadn't happened that way. Now he was sitting down with Major

Green to deliberately plan to kill at least five men. It was shattering.

Green, too, felt bitterness. As always, it wasn't until something struck home that you could get anyone to move. He felt sorry for the pain Manchester felt. It was terrible to lose your ideals and find out the wild animals you keep feeding by hand are never to be trusted, that one day they will bite it off. At the back of his mind one group kept coming forward. If he'd had to give odds, it would be the fanatic fringe of the PLO, Black September.

"One thing, Jerry, and get this straight. Once I put these people on the hunt, there will be no way to call them back until it is over and either they or the terrorists are dead. Once this begins there will be no way to stop them and they'll assume anyone who tries is their enemy and kill them too.

"All information contacts will be run through me and I will be the only one they speak to. In addition, all special equipment will be delivered by my people. You arrange to send it to where I say with no questions and I'll see the hunters get it.

"Now, you've started this shit, but I promise you and the rest of your liberal, egg-sucking do-gooders that by the living God I will not stop my people and if anyone tries, then you will have me and mine to deal with. I'll blow the sheets off all of you, friends or no friends. Now, do you read me and accept this? If so, we'll get on with it. If not, take your fat grieving ass out of my chair and go back to Disneyland."

Manchester was stunned. What he was setting loose might be more than he bargained for. But there was no going back now. He was committed.

"All right." He rose from his chair. "Put me in the bag. Let's go for it."

FOUR

ROSSEN WAS WORKING THE DOOR GUN, SENDING controlled bursts into the roof of the jungle below, returning fire on the pinpricks of light which winked at him through the green of the jungle. Beneath them, in a clearing too small to permit the Bell 412 to set down, a patrol which had been ambushed waited for their wounded to be taken out.

Tomanaga shook his head, yelling at Rossen. "There ain't no way to get down to them!"

The overworked Bell 412 didn't even have a power winch, thanks to Mr. Carter's cutoff of replacement parts and supplies from the States. With that they'd have been able at least to get most of the wounded out, before their asses were blown out of the sky.

It had only been an hour since they'd got the news at Santa Cruz del Quiché. Teniente Irwin Sagusteme was heading for his chopper when

he saw Rossen and Tommy coming out of the
officer's mess.

"Either of you guys a medic?" he yelled,
knowing the answer. Tommy and Rossen had
both received extensive first-aid training over
the years, to the point where they could do an
IV cut-down or treat most gunshot or shrapnel
wounds. They'd had years of experience.

"Yeah, Irwin, you know both of us can handle it. What's coming down?"

Sagastume, whom they called Sock-it-to-me
most of the time, didn't stop moving. "We got
some wounded and there's no one left here to
go out with me."

Tomanaga nodded at Rossen, then yelled to
Sagusteme: "Give us five and we'll be with you.
But you better tell your doorgunner to stay
behind; we'll take that. If you got more than
four or five you won't be able to carry the
load."

Tommy took off to their quarters at a run and
grabbed their med kits. The Guatemalan Army
was so low on supplies that women's sanitary
pads were being used as battle dressings.
Worked fairly well too.

Tommy snatched up some other gear and a
couple of rifles. They had a fair selection of
arms to choose from—and a basic load of
ammo—and double-timed it back to the chopper, whose blades were just starting to kick
over. Handing the gear up to Rossen, he hauled
himself inside.

The regular doorgunner didn't look at all disappointed at missing this run. He'd flown with Irwin too many times. The thin intense man in flight coveralls always seemed to find the action, but so far luck had been riding with them. But you never knew when that would change.

As soon as Tommy was on board they lifted off; tail slightly higher than nose, they rose above the camp to altitude and headed for the mountains and into the badlands. Rossen filled Tommy in on what Sagusteme had told him.

"They got a patrol of about twenty men out there. Stumbled into an ambush, took some casualties, but haven't been able to break contact. Right now they're just holding till we get their wounded out. If they bug out now, the wounded would have to be left behind."

That was something which always ate at a soldier's guts. To be left behind, alone, cut off. It was one of the big boogeymen of war.

As soon as they were clear of the camp, Rossen tested the gun, an M-60 which was older than its regular gunner. Before firing, he checked the ammo with Tommy's help, making sure none of the brass was out of line. One casing sticking out a sixteenth of an inch more than the rest could cause a stoppage. Once he was satisfied with the ammo, Rossen chambered a round and fired three short bursts from the weapon. It was working, for now.

Rossen didn't like flying choppers even when

they were in the best of condition, and this one had seen more than its share of service. It had been hit enough to give the maintenance chief bad dreams every time it went out. Rossen didn't know that, which was just as well.

They got up to about nine thousand, which was nearly max for the old bird and just barely enough to clear some of the mountains—but not all of them. The standing joke was that when the guerrillas wanted to take out a chopper, they would climb up to one of the volcanoes at ten thousand feet and throw rocks down on the bird. Santa Cruz was somewhere near eight thousand feet and the twin turbines, which should have been sent to a rest home five years ago, did their best to keep them up in the thin air.

They passed over Nebaj, a small Indian village at the end of the road, which many considered the last government strong point before Playa Grande on the Mexican border. From here on, the boss of the country was whoever had the most guns and was in the field. Lately, the Gs—the guerillas—had been gathering small bands together for more concentrated ambushes, raids in parties of two hundred or more, which usually gave them the right odds since most patrols were only platoon strength.

Past Nebaj the country became more rugged. Less evidence of human life, fewer cleared or terraced patches of ground where the local Indians, of ancient Maya extraction, planted their fields of corn and beans. Within minutes, they were in thick, hard terrain. Little visibility on the deck. Irwin was trying to raise the platoon commander on the ground and not having much luck.

Inside the cabin, wind whipped at them, and the roar of the whirling blades made it seem as if they were flying inside a vacuum cleaner. The roar muffled nearly all sounds as they drove over the tops of forests, which were not as green as they would be in two or three weeks, when the rainy season began. They could see several plumes of smoke rising from the mountains and the sides of volcanoes. Some were forest fires which no one could get to to fight; the others came from vent holes in the sides of the volcanoes which rose up to touch and sometimes overpower the clouds.

Tears welled up in their eyes as they strained to see beneath them. Irwin yelled back to them. With hand signals he told them he'd made contact with the patrol and they were only a few minutes away. The time was 9:15 in the morning. If they didn't have any problems, they should be on their way out by 9:25 at the max. If they didn't have problems.

Irwin kept his eyes on the edge of the mountainous green horizon. A plume of smoke rose suddenly a few degrees to port. Smoke grenade. That was where his people were. He angled over. The change in course cued Rossen to tighten up on his machine gun, preparing

himself. Tommy lay down on his belly with his
rifle, a Cetme—the Spanish-made version of
the German G-3—and got ready, hoping that
Sagusteme wouldn't make any sudden moves
which would slip him out of the open door.
This was your basic chopper; there was nothing to strap in with.

A round came up through the floor, passing
between Sagusteme's feet, then between his
left arm and body, exiting out the Plexiglas.
They were close. He didn't have time to be
afraid, even if he didn't like anything he could
see. There was no clearing, just a small gap in
the trees from which the column of smoke rose
to be blown away, first by the breeze, then by
the stronger whipping blast of the blades. They
were over the site. His mind was on the job.

Beneath them, Rossen could see the patrol
members spread out, returning fire on the
unseen enemy. One small camouflaged figure
jerked up to its knees quickly and threw something overhanded into the brush, then dropped
back down behind cover. A grenade. The
enemy was close. In the center of the clearing
were five men: the wounded. He could make
out a figure holding a radio and making agi-
tated motions with his free hand, to which
Sagusteme was responding.

He saw a winkle of light to his left, and lay
some fire down on it, and then began working
out from the small clearing with controlled

bursts. He wasn't planning on hitting much of anything, just trying to keep the G's fire suppressed until they could evac the wounded and get out.

But there was no way they could set down.

A touch on his back scared the shit out of him. Sagusteme had turned over the controls of the chopper to his copilot, and was standing over him, holding a coil of rope from the bird's utility box.

Rossen thumped Tommy on the shoulder and indicated for him to take over the machine gun. Because of Tommy's missing hand, Rossen would be able to pull more than Tommy could. Hovering at treetop level, they lowered the rope to the men on the ground, who frantically tied one of their casualties in a makeshift sling and signaled for him to be brought up. Meanwhile, Tommy kept the gun working; the chopper was taking more hits now and it was hard to stay on station.

Hand over hand they hauled the wounded man up, one foot at a time, as the machine swayed and bounced. The rope cut deeply into their hands as they strained to get the wounded man up. It was taking too much time. And the Gs were concentrating all their fire on the chopper.

Tommy tried to keep them down, but they were too spread out. Fire was coming at them from at least three sides. There was no way he could lay fire on all of them so they just had to take it. But to stay there very long meant they were going to go down. No doubt about it.

It seemed like it took half an hour to get the first man on board. As soon as they did, the copilot broke off, putting them well above treetop level a click to the south.

Tommy got off the gun and went to help Rossen with the wounded man. A round had fractured the bone just below the knee. The leg was bound with a red handkerchief for a compress over a sanitary pad. The man was going to lose the leg. The handkerchief had been on too tight for too long. He had gangrene. It didn't show now, but it would.

Rossen turned to Sagusteme. "What are we going to do about the others?" Both knew they could not go back and just hover there while they got their asses shot off.

Muscles worked in Sagusteme's thin, handsome face, as tears began to run down his cheeks. They weren't caused by the blast of the chopper blades.

"We have to leave them."

Every warning light on the panel was lit up. It wasn't even certain that they would be able to make it back to base. That was it. Below them, at least four men would die from wounds which should not have been fatal, because they didn't have a simple thing like a power winch.

Rossen hoped all of Mr. Carter's peanuts

would turn to shit in the mouths of whoever bought them.

Irwin let his copilot take them home. His eyes were too full to see clearly. He just sat there, frustrated and helpless, as Tommy and Rossen worked on the wounded soldier in the back. One out of five was all he could think, one out of five. If the patrol didn't take any more casualties they'd probably be all right. A patrol from Playa Grande was making its way to relieve them. And now that the chopper had been on site, the Gs would probably, as they normally did, break contact.

They were going back to Santa Cruz. One out of five.

FIVE

IT HAD TAKEN GREEN TWO WEEKS TO GET THE
data he required from Manchester. During that
time he had twice spotted tails on him. After
the second time, he placed a call to Manchester stating flatly that whoever was on *his* ass
had better get off or the *deal* was off. Then he
hung up.

Manchester reversed a call to the man from
whom he had first received the news about his
son-in-law. The man at Delta Force answered,
and it was his turn to get some bad news.

"Mr. Jones, or whatever they are calling you
this week, I've done some checking on my own.
You know that the Secretary has put me in
charge, probably because I have opposed him
so many times in the past and he wants to rub it
in. No matter. Because of my position, I know
that the FBI and all other agencies have been
pulled off Green. Logically, that leaves only you

and your group of fanatics. Get, and I use his words, 'off his ass or the deal is off.' That, sir, is not a request but an order, and if you think I can't back it up, just try me. You will be back at Fort Bragg, or wherever they found you, in a matter of days, trying to survive long enough to collect your pension. Which, if I have anything to do with it, will be at a severely reduced rank. Do you understand me, you son of a bitch?"

Jones hung the receiver up very slowly, smiled to himself, punched a number, and spoke to the voice on the other end when it answered.

"Get off of him. Break surveillance and pull back. We're going to let this one run free."

Hanging up, he almost wished he was back at Fort Bragg, but for now this was the only really active game in town.

He thought he knew who Green was going to get to do the job, and envied them their freedom from rules and regulations. One day, if he was lucky and, as the man said, managed to drag down his pension, then he just might look them up. They might have some work for him. He had heard Guatemala was a nice place to retire to, and if they were living down there, then there had to be enough going on to keep from being bored to death or sitting around the VFW till your liver rotted away.

Sitting back with a deep wistful sigh, Jones wished he was going with them. But if he couldn't go, at least he had the satisfaction of putting them on the trail. Anything they needed that he could do or get for them he would see was done. Now it was time to mend fences. He would fly out to Colorado and see Green in person. He was an old soldier too. If anyone would understand his reasons for wanting to be in, he would. Maybe he'd let him help a bit. If he had this called right, the Shooter and his nisei sidekick, Tomanaga, were going to need all the help they could get.

The following morning Jones was at the reception desk waiting for Green to see him. When he was admitted, Green looked up from his desk, pushed his glasses up to rest at the edge of his remaining hairline, and eyed the man. It wasn't hard to figure. He had the look. He was a soldier now or he had done a lot of it one time or another. That made him a couple of points in Green's book. If he wasn't an asshole soldier they might get along. The man's call to him had been interesting enough in what was not said for Green to invite him up.

Jones sat down at Green's gesture, giving the publisher time to size him up. Green liked what he saw. Jones was a few years younger than himself; the body had miles on it but was still in good enough shape to worry many teenagers, and the face was strong, well set, good jawline. Nothing out of the ordinary. You wouldn't look twice at that face on the street, but if you did, then you might look a third time before the power behind it registered. It was a face which had been lived in, lived in hard. Slight bend to the nose where it had been broken once, small mounds of scar tissue puffed up over the eyelids, and those deeper lines at the corner of a mouth which knew pain.

It was all right there, enough signs and lines in his face and eyes to show he'd been on the road before and smelled cordite more than once. That was important. When a man had never done any killing or had people trying to kill him, he had no real appreciation of what it meant.

Green knew Jones was waiting for him to finish his surface analysis and give him his grade. If he failed, he'd be shown out with no further conversation. If he passed the first test, the door was open.

"All right, Mr. Jones. You asked for this meet. What's on your mind?"

Jones smiled inside. The door was open, now he had to walk in before he did anything to get it closed in his face.

"Rossen and Tomanaga are going to need a lot of help and I want to give it. I have the manpower and the facilities to give you support in any part of the world outside the Soviet or Chi Com bloc, and there's a few places where we might be able to do something."

Green sat back, put a fresh plug in his jaw. That Jones knew about Rossen and Tomanaga didn't surprise him much. It was a good sign; the man was using his head for something more than a place to rest his crew cut. Making a couple of solid chews, first moving the plug around to get the saliva going, he spoke slow and certain, picking his words.

"Fine. But first you come clean with me." He paused, spat in his cup, locking his eyes with Jones's over the white plastic-foam lip. "And I mean all the way. If you're up to date, as you seem to be, then you know I still have enough friends left to check you out. So no bullshit, mister, or haul your ass out of here now."

Jones was relieved. The hardest part was over. "All right. You got it. I'm a lieutenant colonel. Regular Army, due to drag in my time in a couple of years. I came up like you did, through the ranks. Two tours in Nam. One with the Fifth Group and a tour with Mac Sog. We were there at different times and I had a different name then.

"I am now the executive officer for Delta Force, which you know gives me access to a lot of data from other organizations in the counterterrorist business. I'm the one who put the bug up Manchester's ass and got him moving. He doesn't, by the way, think very much of me or my group."

That didn't bother Green. In fact, it was a recommendation. "What about your commanding officer? Does he go along with you getting involved with us in this thing? You know it will probably get very messy before it's done."

Jones leaned over. For the first time, Green got a look at his eyes, hazel with dark gold flecks, the eyes of a poet with an iron core behind them. Jones's voice dropped low. "By God! I hope so. I want it so fucking messy those raghead sons of bitches will think the world has fallen in on them. I want them to bleed out of every pore in their bodies and feel fear with every breath they take awake or asleep. I want Tomanaga and Rossen to kill every one of them that they get in their gunsights. And I want, more than anything else in my life, to at least be able to think I helped them to do it.

"As for my boss, he thinks I'm a bleeding-heart liberal and Marxist sympathizer. He just doesn't want to know anything, in case he is brought in for any kind of a hearing later. I'm the one who'll take the fall if it comes to that. That way, we can leave the Force, if not clean, slightly less contaminated, so it can continue to function."

Those words, more than anything else, made Green settle things in his own mind about this man called Jones. "Okay, you're in. But you can't do it halfway, it's all or nothing." Green knew he was going to need a lot of help and he didn't really feel that he could rely on Manchester once the killing started. This man was different. "If you can take over the job of contact and supply for me, *and* keep me informed all the way, then you're in!"

Reaching across the table, Jones held out a

strong hand. "You got it, Mr. Green. All the way," he said, using the old airborne trooper's phrase, a code word from the club.

For the next three days Green turned the operations of his office over to his staff. They grumbled a bit, but were used to his absences and had learned to carry on when he was gone on one of his frequent trips to trouble spots around the world.

He and Jones went up into the mountains to his ranch. There they went over the things they had: intel reports from half a dozen countries; analysis profiles of the terrorist mind from think tanks in Arlington, Virginia; and the pictures, as well as one piece of videotape taken when the terrorists murdered the ten hostages. These had been computer-enhanced and now had a great deal more clarity than the originals. Two faces were clear: the Oriental and one of the Palestinians, whose handkerchief mask had slipped for a fraction of a second. On the original tape it went by so fast that it was hardly noticeable, and even in slow motion it was impossible to make out any distinct features. But with the space age tech of NASA, it had been possible to capture that fleeting second and freeze it and blow it up to where it was no worse than a normal Kodak snapshot taken by a teenager.

They had faces on two of them to work with. It was a good start.

Now it was time for Green to place his call to

Guatemala and run down Rossen and Tomanaga. He used the only number he had: the one for the Europa. He had used it earlier to confirm they were somewhere in the country by asking Freddie if they had been getting their complimentary copies of his magazine, which were sent to the Europa's address in his care. If anyone knew just where they were, it would be Freddie, their best friend in the Central American country which rested just south of Mexico and north of Honduras and El Salvador.

Green had waited till now because he didn't want to call them in early and have things go bust. It wouldn't be fair to them if they had something else going; if he called, they'd come. That he knew. They always had and he had never let them down. They would come and when they did, the dying would begin.

The dial tone in his ear was replaced with a voice saying, *"Bueno, Restaurante Europa, quién hablas?"*

Green smiled. "Hello, is that you, Freddie?"

SIX

THEY DIDN'T LIKE THE CAR RIDE BACK FROM THE 22nd Military Zone HQ at Santa Cruz, high in the mountains of Quiché, twenty-plus clicks north of Chichicastenango on the road to Nebaj. They had been on site too long. If the Gs had their shit together they could be ambushed.

When they were to be pulled out, the commanding officer, Colonel Lima, a tough, handsome, strong-faced man with pepper-gray hair who had as many hours of combat patrolling as any of his sergeants, had promised them he would arrange for a light plane to come in and get them. But maybe, because the course was being cut short, the Gs wouldn't be ready for them to leave by ground transport. He and Tomanaga had spent the last two weeks on a contract to train snipers for the Guatemalan

Army. It was not unlikely for the bad guys to want to take them out.

Rossen settled the Galil assault rifle on his lap. It was brand spanking new and smelled that way. He would have preferred an M-14, but this had a short barrel. Easier to use if they had to fire out of the windows, and it spat out rounds at a rate to satisfy the most wasteful shooter. If they were ambushed, Rossen's rifle and the one Tommy had in the back seat of the Toyota Land Cruiser would be of more value in the opening seconds of the ambush—and that was all they would probably have. If a mine was laid, then even the armor-plated Toyota wouldn't do them much good. If the mine was placed right, they'd probably end up going down one of the cliffs for two or three hundred feet.

Along the road, Mayan Indians dressed in the fine-quality *típico* weavings for which they were famous moved slowly, steadily, next to the blacktop, ignoring the screeching of cars behind them and the honking of frantic horns. They went their own way oblivious to the modern traffic passing them.

Tommy had remarked more than once that they could have taught the Buddhists something about fatalism. They didn't seem to be aware of, or concerned about, the conflict in the hills around them. They had the same stoic acceptance of that which they could not change as he'd seen on faces in Africa, Vietnam, Cambodia, and Laos.

The men wore straw cowboylike hats that wouldn't have been out of place in Dallas or Nashville, as their women walked behind them, wearing the bright handwoven skirts and blouses which identified the *departamento* they were from. On their heads, the women balanced with practiced ease bundles of goods bought or traded for in the central market in Chichi. Tommy didn't know how they did it. He'd once seen a woman with an oxygen tank balanced lengthwise on her head, walking down the streets of Guate and talking cheerfully to friends. The tank was as long as she was tall, and probably weighed more.

They passed through the narrow winding roads of Chichi and headed for Los Encuentros, the junction where the road split off in three directions. One went down the mountains over two thousand feet through Sololá, where an army convoy was ambushed the previous week, to the clear mountain lake of Atitlán with its three magnificent volcanoes. The second was the Pan American Highway leading north to the border of Mexico, and the last was their road, heading back down the mountains to Guatemala City.

For all the risks, they didn't like having to break off the job at Santa Cruz, but the call was urgent and they knew the colonel wouldn't have asked them to come in if it hadn't been something urgent.

Still they'd done good work. The Guatemalans were good soldiers and learned fast. Rossen and Tommy had gotten them through most of the basics and had been in the stages of fine tuning their shooting. They'd been able to cut the course down quite a bit, since there wasn't any real need for the shooters to have to deal with artillery fire direction and a number of other standard courses that Western world snipers had to be familiar with. Their course had been primarily shooting and patrolling, escape and evasion, and the use and care of their equipment. Primarily for morale, Tommy had also given them a quick, ten-day course in basic self-defense.

The side trip with Sock-it-to-me had not been on their agenda. They didn't go out on very many combat operations. The brass was too afraid the Gs would get one of them and use it for propaganda. You know the kind: bold headlines reading PROOF, AMERICAN MERCENARIES IN GUATEMALA.

The Toyota squealed its wheels as it made the turn outside Chichi, where a few months earlier an overloaded bus had gone over the side. There was a marker at the accident site engraved with the names of the thirty or so people who had died, along with a large number of crosses erected by the families of the dead. From the road leading from El Rancho in the Oriente to Guatemala City—some 120 kilometers—they had once counted more than 120 of those macabre markers. The roads in Guatemala were, so far, more dangerous than the guerrillas.

In the back of the Toyota, Tommy watched through the side window as the tall pine forests became a bit more tropical, as ferns gave way to more palms and tropical plant life.

The tinted windows of the bulletproof vehicle cut much of the glare as the heavy machine with its armored panels tore down the hills, past the village of widows, then into Chilmaltenango, the last stretch before San Lucas and into Guate. The four-hour drive seemed longer, but after they reached the valley plain outside Chimaltenango, they relaxed a bit. If the Gs were going to hit them, they would most likely have done it in the hills between Los Encuentros and Chichicastenango. Here it was too open and there were too many National Police and Mobile Army Units patrolling. It would have been harder for them to make a hit and get away in broad daylight, but that did not mean that it couldn't happen. They relaxed . . . but not all the way.

Their overriding thoughts, though, were about what Green had in mind for them. Whatever it was, he had a bug up his ass.

Turning off the Periferico, their driver took them over the bridge onto Ninth Street, then turned left to Eleventh; a right, and they were in front of the Europa, where Freddie plied his trade as bartender, money changer, travel agent, and generally sympathetic ear to his mixed bag of customers—gringos, Germans, limeys, Guatemalans, and Spaniards.

For a restaurant as small as the Europa was, it had an amazing variety of types go in and out its famous doors, on which were the words ENGLISH SPOKEN in neat printer's block letters, and under that, in shakier script where Freddie did the painting himself after a bad night with Johnnie Walker Red, BUT NOT UNDERSTOOD.

The driver opened the rear of the Land Cruiser so they could get their kit out. Giving them an offhand salute, he sped onto Avenida Sexta, turned right at the Piccadilly Restaurant, and headed back up into the hills to Santa Cruz. He didn't want to make the drive back into the mountains at night.

Their exit didn't attract much attention; they were regulars at the Restaurante Europa, and they had changed back into civvies at Santa Cruz. No one at Freddie's had ever seen them in uniform and probably none ever would. Like most of the customers, other than the few spooks and would-be spooks who dropped in now and then and were easily spotted by the regulars, Freddie's customers minded their own business. They speculated, but kept their conclusions to themselves.

Those that did pry a bit more than was advisable were informed politely but firmly by Freddie that it was best if they didn't stick their noses too far into the business of the tall American and his one-handed Japanese-American partner. Most were able to accept this good advice without rancor, but as always, there would be one or two who had to learn the hard way.

Freddie saw them coming and set two shooters of Johnnie Walker Red for them, even though he knew Rossen hated the stuff and claimed to drink it only because he was a masochist and it was the easiest way of hurting himself he could think of.

Tommy and Rossen waved casually to Wolfgang and Milo, who were at one of their interminable games of chess, with Milo speaking nonstop about his ex-wife's relatives in Peru.

Wolfgang ignored the ramblings completely and concentrated on whipping Milo's ass on the board. Milo, as usual, went through what appeared to be his compulsory bout of oral exercises, until he saw that Wolfy had him sewn up. Then would come the customary thump of his small fist on the table, to Wolfgang's great satisfaction, and Freddie would bark at Milo to "knock that shit off." Milo would, as always, apologize, and he and Wolfgang would square off for another contest.

"Hey, Sam, Tommy. See you got the message." Freddie was German, but spoke English with a strange southern accent which could fool anyone except another southerner.

It was he who had relayed the message from Green and brought them back down from the mountains of Quiché. That was another of his many and varied services. He was the best answering service in Guatemala, speaking German, English, and Spanish with equal ease.

Milo was starting to get excited again. Freddie's mustache bristled as he leaned over the bar.

"Knock it off, Milo." Chastened, Milo shrank one or two inches beneath his normal five seven and tried to concentrate on the game.

"How is it in the hills, my friends?" They weren't too concerned about Wolfgang; he was all right, a lantern-jawed Austrian engineer who'd been in the tropics for many years. He moved into the Sicilian defense, which he knew would piss Milo off, and lit up a cigarette, tapping it delicately but firmly into his cigarette holder as he winked at Tommy as if to say, "Got him again."

Rossen turned back to Freddie, looked at the Johnnie Walker Red with a jaundiced eye, thought what the hell, and tossed it down, making a grimace of distaste. "Goddamn it, Freddie, when are you going to get any Jack Daniel's in here so I can stop drinking this fucking kerosene?"

Nonplussed, Freddie replied with Aryan superiority, "When enough of you goddamned southern boys come in here to make it worth ordering!" Satisfied that he had bested Rossen, he repeated, "How is it going? I have heard there are some problems around Nebaj."

Rossen kept his voice down; there was no need to advertise, even if Wolfy did have a vague idea of what they were doing. "Looks like we got a crazy working up there. Not much information on him yet. But he's been doing some pretty bad things."

As always, Freddie was one of the few who never left well enough alone. He was cursed with overweening curiosity, and had to know more about everything than anyone else. He was one of those Germans who, if you asked them the time, would tell you how to build a cuckoo clock.

"Not now, Freddie. Maybe later." Freddie touched the side of his nose with his finger, indicating that he understood it was very hush-hush and not to be bandied about where idle ears might overhear. Pouring another shot to keep the mood of confidentiality going, he leaned over the bar, mustaches bristling electrically with anticipation. "Do you have any idea what Major Green wants from you?"

Exasperated, Rossen snapped back, "You should have been a police interrogator. No, we don't. Just what you told us over the phone."

Rossen checked his watch; they still had about an hour until Green would place another call to them from his office in Colorado. Maybe they'd find out what was going on. Then again, maybe they wouldn't. Green was pretty tight-lipped most of the time. But if he wanted them, they'd go. They always did.

SEVEN

THE FLIES WERE INCREDIBLE, AN INSEPARABLE part of the camp's life. They were everywhere, in everything; your food, your ears, they swarmed to cover every draining pore which opened under the beating sun of the Libyan coast. Perhaps the only thing worse were the men whose unwashed bodies swarmed together several times a day as they worked themselves into a fervor of righteous hatred against all who opposed them, their Kalashnikovs waving in the air, hoarse voices screaming prescribed slogans mindlessly.

Life in the so-called refugee camps of the Palestinians was a great deal less than pristine, approaching conditions which Yoshi found almost unbearable. He could withstand almost any physical torture, but his life among the unwashed was almost more than he could bear. It tested every fiber of his soul to endure each minute.

For Yoshi Tomanaga the adulation received after the Germans agreed to their demands was almost an insult, as if one did this for the praise of lesser beings! The two weeks since they had been taken to the PLO camp outside of Tripoli had been incredibly dull. To his erstwhile, if ignorant, compatriots in the adventure it was a glorious moment. They had once more beaten the Western powers and held the world to ransom.

Yoshi had asked for permission to leave the camp and return to the East where he felt more at home, but this had been denied him, because of the pictures of him which had been plastered over the front pages of every paper in the world. He would have to wait a couple of months before being moved, until, perhaps, he was forgotten, replaced by another face. With reluctance he settled down to wait it out in the faded olive-drab tent which served as his quarters.

His only comfort was his copy of the *Go-rin-no-sho*, the *Book of Five Rings*, which he had brought with him in his flight bag. The writings and thoughts of Musashi, Japan's greatest samurai and poet, comforted him in this desert of intellectual and spiritual desolation as he tried to use the experience as another test of his will.

To ease his nights, when the temperatures

dropped from boiling to just over freezing, he cast himself back to the times of glory when men knew their value and measured it in their contempt of life, even to the rejection of the value of their own. Purity was within oneself. The fleshly shell which housed the soul did not matter. Therefore, he would endure this horror without complaint. He would turn it to his advantage, making it a positive experience by which he would be that much closer to his ideal of purity of self and mind. Purity was all!

"This is pure bird shit!"

Rossen laughed as Tommy wiped off a glob of white slime with a green core from his shoulders. "I told you when we were here last time, not to walk under the fucking trees." The birds had roosted, as usual, in the large spreading branches of the trees lining what they called Bird Shit Square. Thousands of them came each evening to sit on the branches and scream, cackle, coo, and drop their loads on unwary passersby. Each successful bombing strike seemed to be saluted by another round of screeching from the observers in the branching galleries—and the more experienced Hondurans who observed the episodes. This time they had nailed Tomanaga fair and square.

Cursing the scummy birds, Tommy hurried out from under the spreading branches, lead-

ing the way out of the free-fire zone and over a
block to the Hotel Prado, where they were to
meet with Green.

They were staying at a smaller *pensión* two
blocks down from the Holiday Inn, past the
strip club on the right side of the street. They
could have stayed in one of the better hotels,
but Green thought it best if they kept a lower
profile. Which was ridiculous: How could a
gringo over six feet tall and a one-handed
Japanese with a steel claw remain inconspicu-
ous in a country where there were few Orien-
tals and not very many locals who stood over
five six or seven? But if that was what Green
wanted, okay, they'd go along with it. He was
paying the freight.

Stepping through the lobby door, they received a quick look from the desk clerk. He
remembered them. They had been here once
before, now they were back. They had caused
no trouble the last time they visited, but they
had the look of it about them. As he had done
before, the clerk made a note of their time of
arrival and whom he thought they might be
coming to see. He was a bit disappointed when
they took the stairs; he couldn't tell for certain
which floor they would go to. But that did not
matter too much: If he had to make a bet, they
would be visiting the other American, the one
who had checked in earlier this morning, coming in from Miami. Now all he had to do was
wait. Someone would tell him something and

he would have that something to sell. The buyer was not important, only the money. One survived in this poor land by not taking sides too early and giving equal service to all. All, that is, who could pay for it. Or as occasionally happened, and this must be considered part of the risk factor, if they had no money, then who, at the moment, had the gun.

Green opened the door wide and, before greeting them, cast a quick glance right and left down the hallway. Then he ushered them inside before clasping each of them around the shoulders, Latin fashion.

"By God, it's good to see you two dinosaurs still alive and kicking!"

Slightly embarrassed at the display of affection, Rossen wriggled free of the embrace, saying ruefully, "When you're glad to see us, I know that we're about to step in shit. In fact, a load of it fell from heaven tonight." Tommy grimaced and looked automatically at his shoulder, where a pale shade of grayish white rested in contrast to the dark blue of his sport shirt.

Green laughed as he poured them each two fingers of Jack Daniel's. "Looks like the shit birds in the park got to you before I did."

The room was basic: bed, small sofa, desk with a wicker-back chair, and a black-and-white TV on the desk, to which Green had hooked up his portable VCR.

"Before I tell you anything, I want you to see this clip. Then we'll talk, all right?"

Tommy and Rossen nodded their agreement as they concentrated on the Jack Daniel's. It had been a long time since they'd locked gums on anything but the scotch served at Freddie's.

Cutting the overhead light, Green left only the bedside lamp on and started the tape rolling. The drinks were forgotten as the first segment came on. Green's voice came over the sound on the tape.

"One of the agencies got a man in there with his video camera. We've also inserted a few single shots which were taken by a free-lance." The cameraman had zoomed in on the doorway of the aircraft. The figures were small, but with the enhancement of NASA were incredibly clear.

They saw the first man brought out, the exchange of looks between him and the Oriental, then the bullet to the back of the skull. The camera tracked the body as it slumped and fell face forward down the ramp. Then one after another the passengers were brought out to die. All of the killings were done by the Oriental.

Twice the camera came back to his face; he was the only one unmasked except for the brief moment when the scarf covering the face of another slipped for a second, then was pulled back up before Tommy or Rossen had a good chance to look at him. But they knew that stills could be taken of anything they might want to look at later—if Green hadn't already had it done.

Rossen heard Tommy suck in his breath, something he did whenever he was startled or bothered. Glancing over, Rossen saw his friend's face frozen, set rigid, another sign of deep trouble. He had gone Asiatic, drawing everything back inside himself. He had seen something on the screen, or someone. The previous setup had been one of the single shots dubbed on the tape; the one of the Oriental. But this was not the time to ask about it. Tommy would tell him or not tell him in his own good time, and if he chose not to speak about what it was he'd seen, that was his business.

Green stopped the clip, put the winder in reverse, and waited for them to speak.

"We heard about the hijacking and the killings some time ago. So what's new? They got away with it again," Rossen said, taking a short sip of the sweet sour-mash whiskey.

Green stuffed a fresh wad into his cheek. "What's different is this time they want to go after the bastards. Go all the way!"

Glancing over at Tommy, Rossen could see he was pale, a slight tremor running through the shining steel of his hook. He was exercising incredible control, saying nothing. Turning back to Green, Rossen asked, "What do you mean all the way?"

"They want them dead, and anyone who gets in the way is considered a legitimate target. No restrictions at all. You will have help with whatever equipment you need, papers, documents, everything will be supplied. No holds barred. We, and I mean we with big letters, want them dead. All of them. And I want you two to go after them. As for money, this could be your retirement plan if you want to push it. As I said, it's all the way; they'll pay for it. I know the dollars aren't the most important thing for you, but you might as well get it if it's there. God knows, if you pull this off, you will have earned every cent of it."

Rossen finished the last of his Black Jack and turned the glass over, setting the slightly damp rim down on the table.

"We feel the same way you do about terrorists. But are you and your friends certain that you want it done this way? It could"—he used Green's earlier words to Manchester—"get very messy."

Walking over to them from the VCR, Green bent over, his face close to Rossen's and Tommy's. "The messier the better. We are not going to have another chance like this. Right now, the green light is on. For God's sake help me use it. For once we can hit back and no one on either side of the pond is going to object. Everyone is behind this one. The Brits, Germans, Israelis, even the French, have gotten off the fence. Go out there, run them down, and do what you do best!"

Green went back to sit down on the edge of his bed, his hands trembling. Looking from his face to Tommy's, Rossen shook his head slowly, as if not knowing what to do or say. Overhead, a moth tried to force its way inside the shell of a forty-watt light bulb, trying to get closer to the source of the light which would destroy him if he ever reached it.

This was it. The big one. Perhaps that's what bothered him about it. The job was too open, no restrictions. It would be easy to get carried away and get sloppy. Civilian casualties, people who weren't involved, just unlucky enough to be in the vicinity when the shit went down. If they took the job, they'd have to be careful not to let the freedom to kill carry them to extremes, where expedience took the place of selectivity. And there was Tommy. What had he seen on the tape that bothered him so much? The Oriental?

"Do you have any ID on the terrorists yet?"

Opening the drawer of the table by his bed, Green handed Rossen three large manila envelopes. "What we have to date is all here. We think we have an ID on the one whose mask slipped, but that's all. As for the organization behind the hijacking, it's Black September."

Rossen opened one of the envelopes. Inside were several photos taken from the video and enlarged to 8 by 10, with the concentration on the faces. Rossen handed them one by one to Tommy and waited. When the one with the enlarged face of the Oriental was handed to him, Tommy's expression locked down even tighter, the muscles at the sides of the jaw working under his smooth skin. Rossen could see the pulse pick up speed, pounding against the thinner flesh of the temple. This was it. Tommy knew the face.

Softly, gently, Rossen said, "What do you say, Tommy? This one is up to you, all the way. Do we go or not?"

Green, too, could sense that something he didn't understand was going down between them. He kept silent; this was not the time to say anything. Everything would be decided in the next moments by the handsome, calm Japanese-American on whose brow beads of sweat had suddenly appeared as he stared at the photo of Yoshi Tomanaga.

Placing the photo back on the pile of pictures and documents, Tommy didn't look at either one of them. Then bowing his head slightly in the Japanese manner of acknowledging something of import, he hissed between his teeth as Rossen had only heard him do once or twice before in all their years together.

"Ahhh yes! We go for this one. It has become a matter of honor. You handle the details with Green. I know all I need to for now."

He left them alone and went back out into

the streets. Rossen felt sorry for anyone who gave him a problem this night. Something was eating at Tommy, and it would not pay to get in his way. Not that he would start anything, but he would not be nearly as tolerant this night as he normally was.

"All right, Green, let's get to it. We go!"

EIGHT

ROSSEN HADN'T BEEN GONE TEN MINUTES BEFORE an incessant pounding started in Green's temple. At first he considered suicide, then realized it wasn't his head pounding, but the door. Groaning, he pulled his body up from the couch where he had just closed his eyes for a second to rest them and immediately fallen asleep. The empty bottle of Jack Daniel's glared at him with vicious pleasure as he stumbled to the door. Moving to the side of it, he called out hoarsely, *"Bueno, quién es?"*

In a stage whisper from the opposite side of the door came back, "Happy Halloween. It's your favorite spook."

Green shook his head, trying to clear it of the fumes and night spent with Rossen going over the reports and their options. They had come up with a basic format and selected the first strike area just a few minutes before the sun rose over the rim of the mountains surrounding Tegucigalpa. His body was not yet ready to wake up.

Reluctantly, he opened the door and groaned. Jones stood there looking as if he'd just left his tailor and barber. Clean-shaven, neat basic-gray suit, white shirt with a dark satin blue tie and polished shoes. God, how Green hated cheerful people in the mornings. Especially before he'd had a cup or ten of coffee to get his sluggish blood moving again.

"Come on in." He held the door open to admit the Delta Force exec. "We got a few things to go over."

Jones knew they were in business from the amount of time Green had taken with Rossen after Tomanaga left. His people reported that Tomanaga had wandered about the center of town for a couple of hours, had two beers, and returned to his hotel, which he did not leave again. Why Tomanaga left he had no idea, but he could feel that the deal was go. All night he had waited for Rossen to leave. He wished he could have set up a bug in Green's room, but if it had been found, it would have blown everything. Instead, he had to rely on another agent in the room across from Green's to keep him posted of the exact moment when Rossen left the Prado for his own rooms.

Before Green could begin to brief Jones,

another knock came. Jones motioned for Green to remain seated and answered the door himself. His man from across the hallway handed him a tray with a stainless-steel pitcher full of rich black coffee and two cups.

Gratefully, Green accepted a cup, sucking down the aromatic, steaming brew. Finally, when blood had begun to move in the direction of his brain, he spoke. "It's on. They'll do it. Now, here's what they need and where they want it. With the time schedule Rossen gave me, you'll have no more than one week to get everything ready and deliver it to Mexico City."

Jones grinned evilly, his Special Forces mind already leaping to the possible bloodbath ahead.

"You mean they're going to hit the PLO at their HQ in Mexico City? My God, that's fantastic. That'll really shake the motherfuckers up!"

Green groaned. It was too early in the morning for expletives. "I mean, you have what they asked for ready for them. As to who they're going to hit, or where, as of right now that's none of your business. You just live up to your end of the bargain. When you're ready, contact me and I'll let them know about the pickup on the gear.

"I also have another list of items they think they'll be needing for future jobs. It might be wise to go ahead and get it ready in advance. That way they won't have to wait."

As he went over the list, Jones smiled a toothy grin—as though he'd just been fed a satisfying portion of raw meat.

"Oh, don't worry, Mr. Green. From their shopping list, I know that I'm going to love whatever they've cooked up. As one connoisseur to another, I just know this is going to be delicious, a taste of something I have waited for for a long time."

Green groaned again. "Good God, man! Do I have to listen to a cooking class this early in the morning? Go away and let me go to sleep. You have what you want."

Content, Jones had started to leave when Green stopped him with "Oh, yeah, one other thing. When you make the first drop, stick a hundred thousand dollars in it. The boys might need some pocket change."

Jones didn't bat an eye. "Why of course, Mr. Green. I should have thought of that myself. Are you certain that will serve their needs for now?"

Green rose to stumble toward his bed, speaking over his shoulder. "If it's not, you can bet your spook ass I'll let you know."

Closing the door behind him softly, so as not to disturb the already slumbering Mr. Green, Jones whispered, "I bet you will, Mr. Green, I just bet you will. And it will be a pleasure to service your account. *Buen sueños.*"

* * *

Tommy was lying on his bed, eyes open and staring at the ceiling, his claw detached and on the nightstand.

"You get it worked out, Jim?"

"Yeah, pretty much," Rossen answered as he began taking off his clothes, eying his pillow with envy and dread. "I think we've put some of it together. After I crash a bit I'll fill you in."

Tommy rolled over on his side, resting his head on his good arm. "He's my cousin."

Half dopey, Rossen mumbled, "Who?"

"The terrorist on the tape. The one who did the killings. That's why I said it was a matter of honor. It is. Family honor. His name is Yoshi. Yoshi Tomanaga. The son of my father's brother. We went to school together for a while in Honolulu, then he went back to Japan."

Rossen fumbled his way beneath the sheets, wishing the *hospedaje* had hot water, and mumbled wearily, "Any way you want it, Tommy. You know that. Any way you want it." Then he was asleep.

Tommy rolled over, too, and for the first time since he'd seen the tape, he closed his eyes and slept. He had said what needed to be said. That was done.

It was past noon when Rossen's eyes slowly opened, fighting the stickiness of a bad sleep. His mouth tasted like shit. His hands shook, the fingers trembling. He wanted a drink. No, he needed a drink, something that he had never *needed* before. Not even during the bad-good old days in Nam, except for the few times when he went on R&R. Now he had been on R&R for months; it had been too long since he and Tommy had any real work to do.

The job in Guate was okay, but it wasn't the same as being in harness. Maybe he did need a shrink. Why was it that in combat he was steady, hands like ice, and out of it he was a fucking mess? No better than some redneck who had nothing more in life than drinking beer on Saturday till he threw up and could say to his buddies later what a great time he'd had.

God! Time was what was killing him. The great enemy, Time. He was running out of it. Every day he was a bit slower, his hands shook a tiny bit more, each second compounding the next. Time. And he couldn't escape it. It was everywhere. The face in front of him. The lines growing deeper each second, the hair becoming more gray, the pale eyes washing out even more.

It wasn't youth he wanted to hang on to. It was the loss of all that made him what he was, and every minute time took more of him away. What would there be left when the sands had run long enough? A shell of a person, a scooped-out form in which once there had been a man.

Time took everything, leaving only . . . what? Fear? What kind of fear? Fear of not being what you once were? Fear of failing those who depended on you? Fear of failing yourself, and finally the ultimate failure of just simply knowing that you were not worth a shit anymore. That was the day when you'd take your pistol, put it in your mouth, and slowly, ever so slowly, take up the slack and blow your fucking brains out because there wasn't anything left of you worth the living. Time!

Oh, my God, I'm tired and frightened of . . . frightened of myself and what I used to be. Can I do it one more time? Will I fail? Oh, God, let me just hang on one more time.

Rossen tried to stop thinking, his pores opening, filling with the sweat of primal fear. He tried to shake it off, but it wouldn't go away. He was terrified. Not of death, but of not knowing what he was to become. The clock had to run out sooner or later, and then what? Either he would be dead, which was not a bad thing, or he would be alive, which could be the worst terror of all. What did you do when you knew how to do only one thing and no one wanted you for it, or you were too old to be worth a damn anymore. What was left?

His eyes went to the pistol on his bed. There was comfort in its cool black steel. That was one thing they couldn't take away from him. When it was all done he knew the ending to his story. It lay there on the bed. His way out of the pain.

The steel of the pistol was comforting in his

hands. Laying the barrel against the side of his face, he could smell the sweet, slightly acrid aroma of gun oil. It was comforting, familiar, friendly. He knew that there was only one thing which could never be taken away from him: his death. He knew how the story would end. How it had to end. All that remained now was waiting for the right . . . time.

Once he reconciled himself to that, the rest became easy. The fear was gone. He would do the job one more time. They would go out, because they couldn't do anything else. They had to go. But for now the fear was gone. Lowering his eyes, he saw that the trembling in his hands had stopped. They were steady, solid workman's hands, ready to do what was required of them. Somewhere, sometime, those hard hands would gently take up the trigger slack and someone would die.

Death! What was death? To some, to kill was an evil second to none. To others, depending on whom you killed, you were a hero or a maniac. What did it all matter in the long run? Mankind was going to hell in a shit can no matter what one did or did not do.

The sound of deep regular breathing brought his half-glazed eyes over to where Tommy lay, his back against the wall. What about him? What had he said? It was now a matter of honor. Tommy was going to have to kill a member of his family. For what? Honor! Now, there was real fear. He wished he could take some of it on himself, but there was no way. Maybe later Tommy'd open up some more and he could help. Maybe not. Whatever came down, he'd be there. To the end of . . . time.

NINE

IT WAS TIME TO BEGIN THE PAYBACKS. THE PRESSURE was on. For the last three days they had stayed put, watching, waiting. It was only a matter of time till their target showed up. That was all—just time. Fortunately, they did not have a deadline on this one. What mattered was the end result. The sooner the better, but there was no rush. This was their fourth setup since they'd come to Mexico City following the Palestinians' trail. In the past they had been unlucky, or their quarry had gotten spooked for one reason or another. But he was here now and Rossen could feel it in his bones. This was the day.

It had been a relief to them when they used the number Green had given them, and within an hour all they had asked for was delivered to them in a van with Miami plates. They never saw the driver, and neither did they care. The goods were there as they requested. Once they had that in their hands, they were in business. It was nice not having to smuggle anything through customs. Here it all was, just sitting there in a van with the keys in the ignition, waiting for them.

Jones watched them from a distance. All of his men were pulled way back. He wanted nothing to spook them, excuse the pun. They had to be given plenty of slack. There was a locator in the body of the van, but he didn't figure it would do much good. Within minutes they would probably transfer everything to a clean vehicle. Still, it was good to keep what tabs he could on them . . . in case they needed some assistance along the line.

He felt the same anticipation he had felt on ambushes in Asia. There was an intangible sixth sense which told you that something was going down, even if you couldn't see it. Something was definitely going down, and he hoped it would burn the PLO's ass.

The letters and calls had gone to their offices in Beirut and Paris. They had been informed by anonymous sources that their asses were now on the line. The next move was for Tommy and Rossen.

Achmed had rejected outright the threats made to them by the as-yet-unknown sources:

phone calls to their offices, letters threatening death and destruction if they did not give up the location and their protection of the free-dom fighters who had performed so heroically.

That kind of threat was what *they* did, not the Americans or Europeans. If it had been the Mossad, that diseased instrument of Israeli intelligence, they would have taken it more seriously, but not from any unidentified source. They received a fair amount of hate mail on a regular basis, but neither al-Fatah nor the PLO would react as the Western powers did to threats of terror. They used it; it was their friend, their weapon, which gave them influence equal to that of the superpowers and made them feared throughout the world.

There were even those, supposedly on their side of the conflict, who were afraid of them, thought of them as being too radical. Such an idea! How could one be too radical, when the future of your people was at stake and a jihad was being fought to liberate the oppressed peoples not only of Palestine, but of the entire Moslem world?

So Achmed thought as he drove to the build-ing which housed the PLO office in Mexico City. It was very convenient that the Mexican government allowed so many dissident ele-ments to use their country as a base.

The Mexicans' reasons for permitting this were their own. It was rumored that an understanding had been reached with them by some influential friends in this hemisphere permitting such organizations to establish front offices as long as no acts of terrorism or subversion took place within Mexico's borders. The PLO, as well as several other liberation organizations, had scrupulously kept to this bargain . . . if there was a bargain. The front offices in Mexico were much too valuable to jeopardize.

He had put the ridiculous warnings far to the back of his mind. There was nothing which could be done to him to make him betray his comrades in the struggle against the Zionists. That was his last thought as his car exploded, the ignited fuel tanks turning him to a cinder inside his limousine. The driver was blown out the door, his suit smoldering, the back of his head on fire as he tried to run on legs which could not carry his weight. He was dragged down by an Oriental tourist who tried to smother the flames—though to some it may have looked as if he were trying to kick the man to death instead. Within seconds, a crowd gathered around the entranceway to the Palestinian People's Consulate, and were pushed back by armed guards who rushed to the scene isolating it from the morbid onlookers.

Two bodyguards shared the fate of the driver, though they were luckier: They were dead before the flames got to them. Bits of metal had entered soft parts of their bodies, wiping out the flame of righteous fervor which swelled constantly within their breasts.

The oriental Good Samaritan had melted back into the crowd, leaving the screaming, whimpering chauffeur to the attention of others. He had finished.

Rossen pulled back from the hotel window, putting the remote-control transmitter back into a small case. It looked exactly like a portable pocket tape recorder, which it also was. He might need it again later.

He spotted Tommy coming through the crowd. Picking up their bags, he left the room. On the other side of the hotel they caught a taxi to take them away from the confusion they had caused.

In the offices of the PLO in Mexico City, the scene was one of anger and fear. In the council room on the third floor, something like madness reigned. The men argued in the Arab manner, with hands and fists raised in outrage, voices rising shrilly, almost as if they were haggling in the marketplace of Damascus over the price of a chicken.

Mustafa Khaled got the meeting under control by cocking the hammer on his Walther PPK pistol. That was a sound all of them were familiar with.

"Enough of this unseemly shrieking, my brothers. Are we women to act in such a manner? We have serious business to deal with.

Let us do so in a dignified manner!'' Mustafa
cast his heavy-lidded eyes over the men at the
council table.

The faces grew sullen but silent at his repri-
mand, though it was hard for these men to
control their indignation. Mexico had long
been a safe haven for them, and now one of
their own was killed by a coward's bomb right
on their doorstep.

Mustafa stood behind the table facing the
others. Here they were safe. The grounds were
heavily guarded by their own men, and observers were stationed around the building for
several blocks to spot any strange faces, and the
windows and entrances were equipped with
the latest in sensing devices. No one could
enter carrying a weapon in any form. After all,
they invented most of the tricks of the trade;
they knew how to protect against them.

Yes, they were safe here on the third floor.
There was no building within two thousand
meters from which one could look directly into
the offices. This site had been most carefully
selected by their security personnel, who were
constantly upgrading their systems. Soon they
would have offices more secure than the White
House.

It was worth every petro dollar of their
investment, and they had paid heavily for it,
nearly twice the market value for real estate in
this exclusive residential district. But it was

worth it. The men here and their work were too valuable to risk.

Mustafa's eyes, resting over a slightly hooked nose set above rich sensuous lips, grew darker as his face hardened. "We have much to discuss, let us get to the business of it like professionals. Now the first thing—" He cast his eyes around the faces to make certain he had everyone's undivided attention.

"As you know, we were notified that an act of this nature would take place. As of yet we do not know who is responsible, but I promise you this: We shall find out and punish them tenfold in the name of Allah, blessed be His name."

He paused to take a sip from a glass of bottled water. A droplet clung to his upper lip. With thick pink tongue he licked it off.

"Use all of our resources. Those of you who have the responsibility to liaison with our offices in Europe, make every effort to locate the agency behind this act. When we find out, then we shall teach them the most terrible meaning of the word *terror*. We shall turn the tables on them and force them to give us the men responsible for this act. We shall not be driven like sheep blindly to the slaughter. We shall not betray our comrades. We are in this together. To the death!"

His words gave new heart to those seated around the table. With men like Mustafa, they knew they would succeed. He himself, before being elevated to position of controller, had been responsible for many successful strikes against the enemy, and had led several himself deep into the heartland of the Zionists to strike at them in their homes. He was a great man. Perhaps one day he would even succeed the chairman, Yasir Arafat.

For the next three hours they went over details of the assassination, trying to figure out who might be responsible. A dozen counterplans were offered, but there was nothing to base them on for lack of information on who had made the hit. All agreed that the first priority was to gain intelligence. Once they had that, then they would be able to move against their unknown enemy. No effort or cost would be spared. Until then, they would take more precautions to prevent a recurrence of the kind of action which had overcome their good friend and loyal comrade, Achmed Nazim.

When at last the meeting came to a close, Mustafa had still not shown them the message taken from the chauffeur's body. That would have to wait. Evening was beginning, the sun setting behind the hills surrounding the city. The lights were turned on as the bureaucrats of the PLO congratulated Mustafa and each other on their irrevocable decision not to give in to the demands of their enemies.

Before leaving, there was one last thing to do together. It was time for prayer. Forming themselves into three short rows, they knelt on the deep carpet as Mustafa's bodyguard opened the window. It had been determined much earlier that this window faced directly toward Mecca. Mustafa knelt, then the rest of the delegation, their heads pointing in the direction of the window, and relishing the fresh air of the sun fall. His mind was clearing itself for the ritual of prayer. It was comforting to lose oneself in the familiar words of the holy Koran, to repeat the ancient words over and over, as his fathers had done before him since the Prophet had risen.

Mustafa knelt, touching his head to the carpet. He called out with his voice and his mind for his God to bless them and their endeavors, to give them strength of faith in His holy name and His promise to strengthen them in the difficult days to come, and, most of all, to thank Him for the promise of paradise which would come to those who had died in His holy struggle against the infidel.

Mustafa's head exploded. Brains, pieces of skull, and all that was Mustafa's identity and memories and future thoughts splattered over the faces of the men about him. The force of the shock wave which erupted inside his skull was sufficient to blow away ninety percent of his head, leaving the jaw hanging by a bloody strip of tissue connected to the junction of the spinal column and the base of the skull.

Rossen put the rifle down, not bothering to try to break it down or even remove the silencer. It was disposable. He followed Tommy down the stairs to the street, feeling pretty good. A 2,120-meter head shot. Not bad. He still had the touch.

And Mustafa Khaled had his reward.

He had gone to paradise.

TEN

On the other side of the building, they caught a taxi to take them to the airport. Not speaking during the ride, they waited till they had paid their fare, had their bags taken to the check-in counter, and retired to a corner table to wait for their flight to Tijuana. Flying in-country wouldn't attract as much attention as going international right after the hit was made. From TJ, they'd just walk across the border into the States, carrying their hand baggage as if they'd just been doing the tourist thing for a day or two in the border town.

From the table they could keep an eye out for trouble without attracting any attention while they waited. Their silence continued until the *mozo* had taken their order and left them alone.

Rossen leaned over and took a pull at his

Tecate. "What was the deal with the driver, Tommy?"

The nisei scratched at an itch on his left leg with the steel hook that served as his hand. "A target of opportunity. I was going to do just as we said and put the message by the car where it would be found. But I couldn't pass up sticking it on the driver's body. That should shake them up pretty good. Anyway, it's over and we've at least started the ball rolling."

Rossen shook his head. "Might have been a mistake. If anything comes down in the future where you're spotted again, they might begin to put it together. Let's walk a little tighter from here on out, okay?"

The flight announcer came on, first in Spanish, then in English, declaring it was time to board the Mexicana flight for Tijuana. They had business to take care of in Los Angeles before moving on. At least with targets this spread out, they had nearly the entire world to pick from for a shooting platform. If one place was too tight, they'd just move on to the next.

Jones put down his newspaper and smiled to himself. Things were going very well. The boys had started off with a bang. Once he'd picked them up in Honduras, it hadn't been too tough to keep a loose line on them. Nothing too tight; it would cramp their style . . . just enough to keep tabs on them.

He'd been waiting for them when they

crossed the border at TJ. He'd given the customs people orders not to interfere with them in any manner.

They probably wouldn't have been stopped anyway, but just to make sure, he'd been waiting for them. They came through the border check fifteen minutes apart. After answering the standard questions—Where were you born? Do you have anything to declare?—they were let through with no further delay.

There were also no questions from the American officials at the border. They were just going along with another government agency with strong connections to the DEA. Therefore, they figured they were on the tail of a mule bringing a load of dope across. Whatever they figured was fine with Jones, as long as they didn't connect them to anything else. It was convenient at times to have access to multiple government agency IDs, all good and easy to verify.

As soon as Rossen went through, Jones moved out, driving a rental car to LA. When they got there, he didn't want them to have to wait around for anything they needed. By God they had done the devil's work the last few days. And that had been one hell of a shot. From one of his people, they'd picked up the Weatherby 300 Holland and Holland magnum with the special loads they had wanted. Then they'd set it up right after selecting their firing site. They had figured out the angles of degree and headed out into the country for the day. At a remote valley in the desert, they had set up a duplicate site to practice the shot, even bringing several panes of glass to simulate what deflections might occur if their target had his window closed.

He chuckled as he slipped the car into gear and headed for the San Diego Freeway. "Go get him, boys. I'm with you all the way. Just keep me clued in and I'll be where you need me, with all the goodies your little mercenary hearts can desire."

It was going well. Rossen and Tommy had a portable scrambler with them, and a number to call which would put them in contact within a matter of minutes. All they had to do was tell the voice on the phone what they wanted and it was theirs, something like having your genie inside Ma Bell's electronic heart.

One of the nice things about the system was that no matter where they called from, the voice on the other end could locate them in seconds. New technology gave them the capability to locate the exact phone they placed the call from. If it was a private residence, the name of the owner of the phone and his address popped up on the computer screen almost immediately.

They had come up with a simple system to make their drops: A vehicle with keys placed in a magnetic holder under the frame would be waiting for them when the order was to be delivered. All they had to do was get in and drive off. When they were through, they could leave the vehicle anyplace they wanted to. Whether it was reclaimed or not didn't matter. A trace on the motor or plates would lead nowhere. Everything, especially the weapons, had been sterilized.

Adjusting his sunglasses, Jones settled back for the drive, switched on the radio to an easy-listening station, and relaxed. God, he thought, it would be good if I could get them into the outfit permanently. It was a good thought. But he knew there was no way they were going to come in. His boss would have a shit fit if he even mentioned it. These guys had been around too long and were too hot. Sooner or later they were going to be brought down, and the Force just couldn't afford to be connected with them officially.

Too bad, but at least he had them now, and they were going to raise holy hell; even if they got their shit blown away, the ripple effect would have enormous value.

Never again would the Arabs feel that they could get away with anything they wanted. They had been hit, and now they knew the taste of what they had been dishing out for the last ten years. It was their turn to wonder and worry about every car that came up in their rearview mirrors, about door handles possibly blowing up in their faces.

And this was just the beginning. He didn't

think the enemy had a clue yet as to who was making the hits. There had been a couple of threats made by the radical branches of the PLO about vengeance and retaliation, but they didn't know whom to hit, and to strike out at random would not be to their advantage at this time. It would only alienate them more from some of the people they counted on to help them. A terrorist attack had to have a purpose. It had to achieve something against a specified enemy. They did not have that now. If they struck out at random, it might backlash.

The world press was already on their asses pretty heavily over the last incident, and some of their aid might be cut off by the Syrians and the Saudis. About the only ones who probably didn't give a shit were the Russians. Anything stirring up crap in the Western world was to their advantage.

Jones felt expansive. When he got into LA, he'd head to a Mexican restaurant in the old town and load up on enchiladas and chicken tacos. That was about the only thing he liked in LA. There really wasn't a good Mexican restaurant in all of Virginia, Maryland, or the Federal District.

Turning off the radio, he moved onto the Santa Monica Freeway, weaving in and out of traffic. He entertained himself by singing: "It's Such a Pretty World Today." Good fucking song.

He'd made good time. Now all he had to do

was check in, give his location, and wait for the boys to give him a call. He wondered who was on their shit list this time. Whoever it was, he'd find out soon enough. But he had been making a bit of a game of it, trying to figure out who the target was by the location and the type of equipment they wanted. He hadn't done badly: He'd called it right half the time.

ELEVEN

SALIM MURADI HAD WORKED HIMSELF INTO A lather. Now that he had assumed the position of controller he had to have results, and the fate of his predecessor hung fresh in his eyes: He had been kneeling behind him that day in Mexico, when his brains had been blown out of the back of his skull during prayer.

"Something must be done! We cannot tolerate this kind of treatment. If this continues it could destroy all that we have worked for. We must not be vulnerable.

"World opinion already is beginning to swing against us. They are actually cheering these unclean dogs on. I have even heard that in Las Vegas, the gamblers are giving odds on who will be killed next and where the killings will take place."

Using all their powers, the Palestinians of

every splinter group began to search out who
the assassins were and who controlled them. A
week had passed and nothing had developed,
except more trouble. One of their fund-raisers
in Los Angeles had been found in the parking
lot of his Wilshire Boulevard condominium
with the back of his skull ripped off. The report
said that it looked as if someone had used a
stevedore's hook to kill him.

Later that same day a phone call had been
made to one of their agents concerned with
youth opinions in American educational insti-
tutions. The voice on the phone had informed
the agent that the killing in the parking lot was
the continuation of a process which would not
end until they were given what they wanted.
The recipient of the call had no idea of what
that was; only those in the Directorate knew
the full demands.

At 7:15 that evening, when he was to address
a number of students and potential supporters
of the Palestinian cause at a private house near
USC, the agent was garroted. The wire noose
had nearly taken his head off. He was number
six.

The press, naturally, made wild speculations
about a secret band of vigilantes out to avenge
themselves on the Palestinians for one reason
or another. Some speculated on secret death
squads run by the Mossad.

It appeared the killers had not made the
media aware of their demands.

A seed of doubt had begun to creep into the souls of several members of the Directorate about the wisdom of keeping Yoshi and his team in Libya. It had even been said that to do so was a sign of fear. One of the other men who had been at the residence in Mexico City, and who was noted for his wisdom in counsel, had stated with a perfectly straight face that "the men should be sent forth into the world, unafraid to do God's bidding. They were not afraid to die. This they had proven on the airstrip at Tripoli. They are, as we are, soldiers of God, fighting in His holy name, for the return of our homeland!"

This wise and courageous man had not himself ever taken direct action against the enemy. Salim Muradi began to seriously consider sending him on the next suicide mission, giving him the opportunity to meet the death which he now so easily offered to others.

After concluding the meeting, Muradi went directly to the Soviet embassy, using all safety measures. Three heavy Dodge vans with bulletproof, tinted glass, and reinforced bottoms left the residence at the same time, each taking a different route to throw off any would-be attackers.

Since the death of Khaled they had all taken to extraordinary precautions. None would now enter a room casually and turn on the lights; first they would make certain that shades and blinds were drawn to cut them off from the outside world. All this and more served to feed the paranoia which they came to believe was not paranoia at all. Someone was out to get them.

After being admitted to the Soviet embassy, and submitting to a search of his person, Salim was shown to the office of the newly arrived Second Secretary. Behind closed doors, they eyed each other with open suspicion.

"And how may we be of service, my dear Salim?" The Second Secretary, Theodorovich Cherny, knew why Salim was there. Offering him a comfortable chair, he asked if he wished tea or coffee, which Salim declined, knowing the caliber of Soviet taste. Instead, he watched Cherny, waiting for him to begin the conversation and open the subject matter for the day.

The man was elegant, well dressed and tailored. Thin long fingers and a sensitive face. Salim thought his nose a bit thin and overly long, giving him the impression it was always on the verge of dripping. The Russian's thin-browed eyes had a touch of the Asian steppes to them. He was obviously of a better class than the workers of his country . . . and infinitely more dangerous. He had arrived in Mexico three days earlier.

The KGB was his master and Salim knew some of his history. Those delicate fingers had caused much pain in the last years. He had been liaison for the PLO for a long time, arranging for their young men to be sent to special schools on the coast of the Black Sea near Odessa, where they learned the fine arts of terrorism.

As always, the Soviets attempted to subvert a number of the students. This was, of course, done under the auspices of the KGB. They had not been overly successful in finding those who would do their bidding and not that of the PLO.

It was a game they had played for years. Those few who fell under the spell of the Russians were not hard to cut out and neutralize. In fact, they had always been careful to preselect some students whom they were certain would fall under the Russians' control. It was much easier to deal with them later. They always were among the front line of casualties in any confrontation. Perhaps one or two slipped through their fingers but that was the price they had to pay for the money, weapons, and training they needed.

"My dear Salim, it appears you have a bit of a problem." He lit a Winston cigarette, puffed it into life, and waited for Salim to pick up the thread of conversation.

"Yes, we have a problem. What I would hope for is that you may be able to assist us in determining the true extent of the threat and who is involved with it."

"Ahh, Salim, my friend. It is good that you come to us for assistance. As always, we are prepared to give whatever aid we can to our friends. I have already made certain inquiries

into the matter. But"—he shrugged eloquently
—"as of yet, we have nothing to report. Perhaps when they strike again, they will make a
mistake. Then with a bit of luck, we will be able
to learn more."

"When the next attack takes place! Is that all
you have to say?"

"What else can I say, my dear friend? We
have nothing to share with you. And I am
certain there will be another attack. As the
Americans say, 'You don't quit when you are on
a roll.' The question is when and where. I
would suggest that all of your truly irreplace-
able people be pulled back to the Middle East
for the next few weeks. You can, of course, use
the pretext of a conference to cover the real
reason."

Salim tried to conceal his irritation and
disappointment. If the KGB did not have any
information, then no one would.

"That is all you have to suggest? For everyone
to turn and run like sheep?"

Theodorovich Cherny tapped out his cigarette. "Why, not at all, my dear Salim. You may
always, of course, stay out in the open and be
killed. Of course, that is, as always, your decision. All we can do at this point is offer advice
in the matter."

Mentally, Salim cursed him with a disease
which would affect his private parts for the
next three generations. "Please understand,
Mr. Secretary—it is secretary now, is it not?"

Cherny was not the least bit affected by Salim's sarcasm. The opinion of lesser beings meant nothing to him. He nodded offhandedly to indicate that it was so.

"Then I presume we have nothing further to discuss at this time, Mr. Secretary, and we must take matters into our own hands for the time being."

Cherny rose to show him the door, saying as they walked across plush carpet, "That is always the best course of action, my dear Salim. Whenever possible, do it yourself. We have always stressed the self-help aspect of our programs to our comrades of the third and dispossessed worlds. Help yourself and depend on your friends."

Closing the door behind the Palestinian, Cherny smiled tightly. *Help yourself, you bumbling sand nigger. If it were not for us, you'd still be picking up camel shit to cook your meals by.*

Salim's thoughts were even less kind as he expanded the disease to cover all members of the Russian's family unto the fourth generation. He would, however, take the Russian's advice and return to the Middle East. Not Beirut; the city was depressing and dangerous. So far, he thought, there had been no attacks made in Europe. Paris would be a good place to stop on his way to, say . . . Cairo. Yes, that was it. Egypt would do very nicely for the time being. Close to Europe and the Arab world. Communications would be easy to maintain from their offices there, and it was much easier to obtain the aid of the authorities when problems presented themselves. The Egyptians were, if not openly on their side, still part of the Arab world and gave them support where possible. Support and sanctuary.

TWELVE

ON THEIR LAST NIGHT TOGETHER BEFORE THEY took separate routes for Paris, Rossen tried to get Tommy to open up.

"You know, I don't much care for this one, Tommy. I'm still afraid it might get out of hand and we'll end up taking out some people who don't deserve it."

He had gone to Tommy's hotel at eleven that night to go over some of their options, but the matter of the Oriental on the tape and 8 by 10s kept eating at him.

"I ain't never pushed, Tommy, but you got to at least tell me that it's worthwhile. Do that much, and I'll leave it alone."

Tommy got off his bed. He still had his shoulder harness on, but the hook was lying on the nightstand. Reaching under the bed, he took out a flight-style bag with the name of an obscure dojo in California. Unzipping it, he took out a long knife in a lacquered sheath: a ten-inch chisel-tipped *nambam-bo*, not the more common *tanto*-style knife which was often used as the companion blade to the Japanese sword.

Unsheathing the weapon, he showed it to Rossen. Ancient-style close-combat weapons weren't his specialty. He was good at hand-to-hand but had no real interest in exotic or unusual edged weapons. A plain K-bar served his purposes well enough.

"That's nice, Tommy. I don't think I've seen it before. You get it here?"

Tommy nodded. "Yes. I picked it up yesterday. I think I'm going to have a need for it."

He made a couple of moves with his hand and the wrappings around the handle fell apart. The *nambam-bo* had a threaded end instead of straight tang. Tommy screwed it into the receptacle which normally carried his hook. It was a vicious-looking thing as it became part of Tommy's body.

"You said you think you're going to need it. Can I ask why?"

"Because the Oriental on the tapes is my first cousin, Yoshi. We played together as kids. He came and stayed with me a while in Hawaii, and I lived with him and his family for two years in Japan. We used to play the Japanese version of cops and robbers or cowboys and Indians by a hot spring near his home at Shuzinji, a bit south of Tokyo."

"I didn't know you had any family left, Tommy."

"With the exception of Yoshi, I don't. My parents died first, then his a few years later. We were both big enough to take care of ourselves by then. But he is still the only family I have, and he's gone bad. I think I know why. But it's not something a Westerner would easily understand.

"Let's just say that things have come down to being a family matter. And that means it is my business to settle it with Yoshi."

He unscrewed the knife and put it back in its wrappings, then into the flight bag, returning it under his bed.

"Promise me one thing, Jim. If it's possible to do it without getting you hurt, let me deal with Yoshi, okay?"

There was really nothing Rossen could say. Tommy hadn't asked much of him in this life and there wasn't any way he could refuse him. He knew that Tommy, though he didn't make much of it, was very much Japanese in some pretty deep ways.

He didn't understand, but he didn't have to. If Tommy said he wanted it this way, he'd go along. He'd go along, but he'd keep a round in the chamber, just to make certain that the game came out right. This Yoshi was a crazy son of a bitch and a stone killer.

He'd been wondering why, in the last few weeks, Tommy had taken more and more to doing *katas*, training exercises, when he was alone. Every time Rossen came around, he'd stop. He couldn't understand it; he'd seen Tommy work out plenty of times before.

It had to be this family thing with him. Something to do with honor. He hoped, for Christ's sake, that he wasn't going to go samurai on him. That was dumb. Karate was fine, but he'd never seen anyone stop a forty–five with a sword, and the gun was certainly a lot faster.

"Ah, yeah, right, Tommy. It's hard for me to understand, like you say. But if that's the way you want it, that's how it'll go down. Just remember one thing, though: You got family. Me!"

Tommy said nothing. That had been as close as Rossen had ever come to him. There was nothing to say about it, so he changed the subject.

"What about France? You think we're going to have any troubles there? They've been pretty tight with the Arabs and PLO ever since they started acting up. Are Green and what's his name—Jones?—sure that they're not going to lay on extra security? If they do, it might make it a little tougher for us to get next to the targets."

Rossen pulled a chair over to the nightstand, glad to change the subject.

"It don't make any difference. If it's too tough there, we move on. We have all the time we want on this one. But from the intel we've been getting with our drops, I don't think they are going to do very much other than pay lip service to the Palestinians for a while. Too many of them want somebody's blood for offing one of their star artists. The fucking frogs are weird. Blow up a plane filled with women and children and they turn the other way. Kill one lousy painter or whatever he was and they want to dust off the guillotine. Strange people!"

Tommy shrugged. "Whatever. If we keep the pressure on them, they'll do one of two things. They'll either catch up to us and do obscene things to our bodies, or they'll throw the terrorists and my cousin to the wolves. Namely, us."

Nodding his head, Rossen agreed with him. "Well, that kind of limits things. But what do you think about all this Palestinian and Jew thing?"

Lying back down on the bed, Tommy rested his head on his bad arm, leaving the other free in case he needed it for anything.

"I don't know. It's one of those there-aren't-any-answers-for things. So they just go on killing each other. But till they do it faster than the others' birthrate, I don't think it's going to wind down."

Rossen felt pretty much the same way. The Palestinians did get a rough deal. When the Brits turned Palestine over to the Jews, they set the stage for war.

The Palestinians were Arabs and that's

whom they sided with. They lost. They lost their homes and lands and now most of them lived like dogs in refugee camps.

Then again, the Jews had claims too. And they weren't going to give up what they called the homeland. They would fight to the end, determined that now that they had come home no one was going to push them out again. There would be no more pogroms or concentration camps where they went meekly to the butcher shops. From now on they would fight.

But even if the U.N. somehow forced them to give it up, what would you do with them? Where were they to go? Would they just become the new Palestinians?

Before Rossen took off for his own hotel, the only thing they had agreed on was that there was no agreement on who was absolutely right in the matter. All they knew was that terrorism as official policy was wrong. If you were going to fight, then fight your enemy. Don't take outsiders and randomly kill anyone who happens to be in the wrong place when a bomb goes off. Or took the wrong plane for a vacation in Greece.

They knew that they themselves were considered terrorists by their targets. Perhaps they were. But they were playing the game by their enemies' rules. *They* had set the stage making it international, without boundaries of land or behavior.

The only restrictions they had were those

they placed on themselves. Both knew that if it got out of hand, they would go out themselves before they'd let innocent people take a fall. Only their targets would die. That was their only rule in the game, but the terrorists didn't know that.

THIRTEEN

THEODOROVICH CHERNY LOVED PARIS. NOT THAT he cared much for Frenchmen. But the women were stylish after the cows of Moscow, and the wine was good, though the food was over-cooked to his taste, and smothered in pungent sauces which he always suspected were more designed to cover the odor of tainted meat than to add flavor. The reports in his hands as he paced smoothly back and forth in the office made available to him at the embassy told him only that for five men the City of Lights had suddenly gone very dark.

He lit up a Winston and settled back into a broad-backed leather chair to mull over the developments of the last few weeks. Five of the officials of the People's Bureaus, as Qaddafi liked to call them, had gone to paradise. All killed; individually in different manners. Right now the People's Bureau was an armed fortress and they were screaming for more police protection. No one went out. All food and beverages were flown direct from Libya.

Cherny laughed hoarsely. That would serve them right: Force them to eat their own cooking. God, that was almost a greater punishment than killing them.

He moved over to the desk, an ugly affair left over from some French period or another, touched the intercom button, and ordered tea. He would be here for some time going over the reports.

Five men dead. Five different methods used. No pattern. Or was the lack of one a pattern? What was the purpose? Obvious: They were methodically instilling fear.

A bomb which takes out five men at once is not nearly as terrifying as five individual kills, all done in different manners. This makes one question if he is next to die. Specifically targeted for death. Not just taking a random chance. To be selected for death and not knowing when or where it would come was a most terrifying weapon, Cherny knew. He had used it himself often enough.

Five men: One shot. One run over with a stolen furniture truck. One with his neck broken in multiple places. Another electrocuted when his hair dryer fell into the tub with him. He never did trust those things.

And last, the autopsy report stated that an edged weapon had entered under the right floating rib to a length of ten or eleven inches, then was moved to the left side toward the spinal column slicing through kidneys, liver, and stomach, and when the slice to the spine was completed, as the blade was drawn out, it severed the spinal cord as well. Internally very messy, but very effective.

The only other item of interest, other than the method used to kill, which was that of a professional, was the lab report speculation that the type of blade used was not a normal butcher knife or one of those pointed semi-useless so-called commando daggers which were so much in vogue at this time. Not at all. This was a different kind of knife. The pathologist suggested a blade perhaps one and a half inches wide with a flat tip to it rather than a point. A razor-edged chisel was the analogy used.

Ah yes, one other item of interest. On the victim's collarbone was a puncture made by some kind of round, curved instrument. Something in the general shape of a baling hook. Now, what could that be and why use it anyway? The knife was the killing weapon. The puncture of the tissue by the collarbone would be painful, but it was not deep enough to do any real damage. Interesting, and that is what made his job bearable.

Five down, how many to go? A tap at the chamber door, which opened to his call, permitted an aide to bring him his tea.

Sipping it after he was once more alone, he tried to put it together. The killings had begun in Mexico. Was that significant? If so, how? Then Los Angeles, now Paris. They were moving.

Where would the next strike take place? He had no doubt there would be another. After all, the killers were on what the Americans called a roll. At this point there was no way to tell.

He had to have a direction. Whoever they were, he wanted them himself. Oh, to be sure he would give the credit away. But he and his superiors would know who was responsible. The ragheads were good for bombs and simple shootings of unsuspecting passersby in the street. But these men, and he was sure there was more than one, were professionals. And good. Imaginative also, which made them more dangerous. They would avoid repeating themselves, except when they thought the enemy would not expect them to.

A quandary. How to get them out into the open? The answer was obvious: Give them a target they couldn't refuse. And what target was that? Why, what they had asked for all along. The terrorists who had taken the plane.

That was what they wanted. Why not give it to them? They would have to go for the offering, and when they did, he would have an opportunity to pin them down. He would have to speak to Qaddafi and the chairman of the

PLO. Perhaps it was time for the killers to be given what they wanted before they systematically killed off what few brains the Palestinians and the Libyans had among them. At this rate it would not take long.

Abdul Sharif was, on the surface, furious at the suggestion that the Libyans give up their protection of brother Arabs in the struggle against Zionist imperialism, but also relieved that it had come from the Russians. If worse came to worst, he could make it known that the brothers were only set loose after tremendous outside pressure from the Soviets.

Not that that kind of information would ever be made public. Now, if the Colonel agreed, it would be taken out of his hands. All he could do was obey orders.

If he'd had his way, he would have thrown them to the wolves long ago. This living in constant fear of assassination was hard on one's system. The few times when he had to leave the grounds, he didn't even wear his kaffiyeh, afraid it might draw the killers' attention.

He'd had nervous diarrhea for the last week. His staff, too, were showing the strain. If he could exert any influence at all on Colonel Qaddafi's opinion, he would in his own way suggest they go along with the Soviet proposal.

After all, the Palestinians were not Libyans.

They were to be used, but not if they ran one's accounts into a deficit profile.

Abdul Sharif and his brother, Basil, who now worked for the OPEC office in London, had both been successful accountants at one time, and still tended to think as if everything could be put on a ledger with neat rows to show profit and loss. If that could have been done, the Palestinian account was definitely in the red.

After Theodorovich returned from his conference with the First Secretary of the People's Bureau, Mr. Sharif, Comrade Cherny thought he had it figured out. All it would take would be a touch more paranoia and Mr. Sharif, bookkeeper Sharif, would suddenly find the bill too high and run to Qaddafi.

He didn't believe the job would be too difficult to set in motion. There were several operatives who were quite experienced in wet operations available to him in Paris, and London was only a short flight away.

Still, to be safe, he would use a cutout and have the job contracted out, with one of his agents acting as an intermediary. That way, if anything went wrong, neither he nor the Soviet Union could be connected with it.

After all, they were supposed to be sympathetic to the Arab cause. To have it known that they had one of their officials killed would not serve to create much confidence in the relationship. Normally, he would not have taken such a radical course, but for some reason this was becoming increasingly important to him. He wanted the hunters. There was nothing on his agenda with even a modicum of the challenge they presented.

FOURTEEN

TERROR STRUCK AT HIS HEART. HE HAD NEVER been a fighter. He had, of course, as was his responsibility, handled the funding for several groups so they could complete their assigned missions. But he had never in all his fifty-two years personally taken a human life.

Always his life had been numbers and administration. Now death stalked him. It was close. He could feel it lurking in every shadow. Every movement at the corner of the eye.

He had the shits almost constantly. Anything he tried to eat sat like hot coals in his stomach. He knew he was getting an ulcer.

The assassins had killed his brother in London: In his own home they had avoided the surveillance, entered and butchered him. That was the only word for it. Butchered. His body had been torn apart. It took over an hour for the police to find his head. When they did, it was in the microwave with his testicles in his mouth. The assassins had cooked it.

Nausea cramped his stomach again. There had been pictures. Not the ones the police offered to show him, with obvious relish, the animals. No, he had seen the ones which had come in the mail, showing his brother's death in graphic detail.

He had been disemboweled, then dismembered. Each photograph showed less of him. Only the blood increased with each new picture. And the last picture! The one showing a meat cutter's saw severing his brother's head from his body had his own name printed on it, and the promise that they were coming for him.

He was to be next. They were coming after him. He had to go home. To Libya, where there was proper security and he could be protected against these maniacs. But should he fly? What if there was a bomb? He knew the killers would stop at nothing until they got him. Then they would do even worse to him.

In his conversation with Cherny, the Russian pig had made allusions that his agency would be available to help eliminate the killers once they were in the open.

He would arrange another meeting. If what they wanted were Hasan and his team, then by Allah he would see that they were given them. If they wanted to hunt and kill, he would let them hunt other killers. That was what they really wanted. Not him!

Cherny was not surprised at the note of urgency in Sharif's ever so slightly trembling voice as he requested the Russian to come to the People's Consulate for another meeting to discuss again the subject matter of their last encounter.

No, Cherny was not at all surprised. He had seen duplicates of the photographs sent to Sharif.

Now he believed the Libyans would do as he wished. He had already had several conversations with the chairman of the PLO, who were nominally in charge of the refugee camp. They also looked for an answer, one which would save them face.

He thought he had it for them. If things went well in the next few days, the Hasan team would be on its way somewhere. He would discuss that later, once he had the chairman and the Colonel in agreement.

After all, who knows? They could be next in this wholesale killing and slaughter of Palestinians and their supporters.

That was an idea. With some regret at the current political timing of things, he had to pass on the idea. Though it would have been a marvelous opportunity for the KGB to make changes in the administration of the PLO and government of Libya, the timing was wrong.

Regretful! When would they have another opportunity such as this present itself?

Jones was worried. He was still in Paris
waiting for the next contact with Rossen and
Tomanaga. On his desk were copies of the
police photographs taken of the corpse of Basil
Sharif—or what remained of it.

Had Rossen and Tomanaga gone off the deep
end? This was a bit more than he could sanc-
tion. He didn't even know they were going to
London. The loose string he kept on them had
slipped away from him four days ago. He had
no idea where they had been or what they were
doing.

He had avoided sending out any teams to
locate them. But if it was them, they'd have to
be stopped. He would have to call in some of
his people and go after them. It was not an idea
which pleased him. These guys were not
spooks, but they had survived a long time and
they didn't do it by being reluctant to kill. He
didn't want to lose any of his men if he could
avoid it. The question now was could he?

He felt his ass loosen up when the call came
through on the scrambler.

Rossen's voice was flat, distorted over the
line, but clear enough so not a word was lost.

"Go ahead, I'm here." He waited to give
them the chance to talk first. It was with a great
deal of regret that their locate system did not

work outside the United States, or he'd have them located and someone on their tail before they could hang up.

"Mr—?" the voice began. Then continued with, "You know we need to have something to call you by?"

Jones said a bit stiffly, "Smith will do as well as any."

"Okay, Mr. Smith. We're checking in to let you know that it was not us who did the job in England."

"How do I know that?" Jones asked.

"Because it's not our style." Rossen continued talking, giving Jones his and Tomanaga's locations during the time of the killing, broken down over a matter of hours, for him to check out, which, if right, proved they could not have been in London at the time Basil Sharif was butchered.

He believed them. And Rossen was right. The method, from what he knew of them, which was substantial, was not their style.

"All right, we'll check it out. Just let me say that, personally, right now, I believe you. But the press is raising hell about it. I'll try to settle down our friends.

"But if you didn't do it, that means someone else did, and they are throwing the heat on you. For what reason I don't know, but it does give room for some speculation. Till I check things out keep on the move and call me back in forty-eight hours. I'll try to have something by then."

Putting down the phone, Jones thought over the idea that someone else had come into the game. From his contacts, he knew the Arabs and Palestinians thought it was the same men who'd done the last jobs. Their asses were tight and they were scared.

Were the new players trying to help them in some way? Or were they just copycat killers? That it could be coincidence at this time was too far out. Sharif had security. This was not an amateur hit and whoever did it was mean. The man had been slaughtered like a sheep ready for shis-kebabbing.

Interesting thought. He'd put out some feelers and see if anything came up.

Tommy asked Rossen when he hung up, "Did he believe you?"

"Yeah, I think so. He's going to check things out. He said there might be someone else involved but he didn't know who or why."

After finishing their call from a public phone kiosk, they went back to where they had rooms in a *pension* which catered to the transit trade. The concierge was used to strange types coming and going. As long as they paid in advance, and twice the going rate, he never asked for papers.

Tommy lay back on the bed in his room. It was a few degrees below basic survival levels:

threadbare covers which one was reluctant to touch under the best of circumstances, forty-watt light bulbs which were sufficient only to keep the room in constant dimness and hurt the eyes if you tried to read, a porcelain water pitcher which they were reluctant to drink from on the one small table which should have gone to the termites before the end of World War II. And no private bath. That was shared with the often less than sanitary other clientele of the *pension* Le Rouge Coq.

"Well," Rossen asked, "what do you think we should do now? Go somewhere else and wait it out for a while? Call Green and see if he knows anything? What?"

Tommy closed his eyes. "Let's just hang in here for a few days till we hear something from what's his name."

"Smith," Rossen told him. "That's what he said to call him."

Tommy grunted "Why not?"

"But until we get something more firm, Jim, I would just as soon stay here for awhile. And if things are going to go to shit, we shouldn't involve Green any more than we have to. Let's just leave him out of it."

Rossen knew why Tommy wanted to hang around Marseille. He had found a *sensei* and was working out with him every free moment, polishing his skills in the martial arts. Something new, though, was the amount of time Tommy was spending practicing kendo, Japanese sword fighting, and he practiced with that strange chisel-tipped knife constantly.

As for Green, he agreed with him. Since they'd been put on to this Smith, there was no need for them to contact him directly anymore. Smith was faster and so far he had delivered everything they'd asked for. They had called Green once while in LA to see if he was being kept posted. He was.

They waited out the forty-eight before calling "Smith" back. During this time they stayed close to their rooms, but not so close that they would attract attention. Tommy went out regularly to his training exercises, which took at least four hours a day, and Rossen hung around the waterfront watching the trade ships come and go.

Like most landlubbers, he was fascinated by the sea but had no desire to be a sailor. He spent hours on the wharves, just watching, smelling the odors that only a seaport can have: fish and spices, grease and rust, mixed with the bite of oil-polluted salt water. The waterfront hadn't changed as much as the rest of the city. It still had the feel to it of times past.

Across the Med was North Africa, where the men they wanted were also holed up, waiting.

Not staying in any one place long enough for anyone to strike up a casual conversation, Rossen just wandered, ate seafood, came back to their rooms when he was ready to, and stayed in.

Each wanted desperately to know what the next call to "Smith" would reveal to them. Rossen didn't think Tommy could be called off this one. If he had to, he thought his one-handed partner would go into Libya by himself to get them. Or, more specifically, Yoshi.

FIFTEEN

"THEY'RE GIVING THEM UP." JONES WAS BARELY able to control the excitement. "I guess the last number was the one that broke the camel's back."

Jones wanted to get back into harness for this one, but knew he couldn't. "Oh, by the way. I checked out your story and everything is five by five. No sweat. Someone else made that one."

On the other end of the line, Rossen felt his gut tighten up. "What do you mean, 'they're giving them up'?"

Jones grinned evilly over the phone. "Oh, don't worry. They are not going to turn them over to us for trial. You are going to have to go and get them. A message was delivered quite discreetly so that it would reach all major intel networks. It came in just an hour ago."

Controlling his own adrenaline rush, Rossen asked quietly, "Where are they?"

Jones answered him with pleasure. "If what we have received is right, they should be about halfway to Bangkok by now. They pulled out this morning. There's a stopover in New Delhi. One of my people will go on board to verify that they're on the flight.

"In the meantime, I suggest you make your reservations and get your asses in the air. I'll be there a little before you. I still have the right to take a military hop now and then. See you in Bangkok. When you get there, check in with me. I should have some more data for you."

He gave them a number to call when they were in-country.

The line went dead. Turning his head to Tommy, Rossen said softly, "Yoshi and the others are on the move. It looks like Bangkok."

Tommy sat up on the edge of his bed. He said nothing except, "Well, I guess we better pack, hadn't we?"

As Rossen was leaving to go to his own room, he turned at Tommy's door to see him place the *nambam-bo* in his suitcase. Something cold ran over his spine, causing a shiver to ripple his body.

"Right, Tommy. I'll book us out on separate flights. Guess you want to get in first?"

Tommy nodded his head. "Yes, that will be fine. Thank you."

* * *

Yoshi separated himself from the others when they boarded the Jordan Alia flight from Tripoli back to Amman, from there with a change of planes to New Delhi, then nonstop to Bangkok. He did not wish to spend the eleven hours, including the change of aircraft, in the company of the Palestinians. He had been punished enough the last weeks.

He had known, of course, of the actions being taken against the Arabs by an unknown group of assassins. It did not take much imagination to put two and two together. Though it had never been said to them directly, they had found out the reasons for the killings. The assassins wanted *them*.

Yoshi had to admire them. It was always somewhat humorous when the enemy used your own tactics against you and won. *Won*. That was not quite correct. They had made a series of moves which appeared to have worked, but the game was far from over.

They had been told, of course, that they were being sent out to prepare for another operation, the context of which would be given them at a later date. They had no need to know any of the details of the forthcoming action at this time.

Yoshi snorted sarcastically as he sipped at a poor grade of tea, served by a less than enthusiastic Jordanian stewardess. *They made up their minds so fast. They didn't have time to think up even a good cover story. Being sent on another operation. Really!*

Yoshi had no doubt that before they reached their destination, all of them would have been identified at least three times. They had probably been tagged when they boarded the aircraft. Still, it would be entertaining to see how things worked out.

Whoever they, and that was still an unknown factor, were sending after them had to be very good. It would be a pleasure to meet someone with a bit of style. It would at the very least be a change from the company he had been forced to keep of late.

Outside the window there was nothing to be seen, only the bare, naked, dry earth beneath. At least he was getting closer to home, to the sacred islands, where even if modern Japan had sold its soul and had forgotten its heritage, he had not.

Soon he would make his death statement, his *zankanjo*. The final word. His protest against the corruption which had stolen the sacred islands away from their heritage and honor, making merchants out of warriors, thieves and car dealers out of princes.

Yoshi closed his eyes and slept as the jet flew high over the deserts. He slept well and deep. He dreamed of another time, when he wore the *mon* of the Kamakiri, the mantis, symbol of courage, on the breastplate of his black-lacquered armor, and fought for the Emperor.

The god-king, direct descendant of Ameratsu, the sun-goddess.

Ah, the great battles he fought and the enemies he slew. By the dozens he slaughtered masterless men of no value. They served only to test the edge of his katana. Great battles where he was always honored by his daimyo by being put into the forefront. The most dangerous position, where death was with every heartbeat and made welcome. Welcome death.

In death was the final purification of the soul, the opening of the gates to the last karma. It was not to be feared or denied. It was to be accepted without fear. But it had to come on one's own terms. In his dreams he could smell the battlefields, the blood rich in his nostrils and his mouth. The taste of copper and salt.

It was good. Kill and be killed. To be samurai. There was no other way.

The stewardess passing out snacks looked down at his face. As with many of his race, it was sometimes very hard to tell how old he was. He could have been in his late twenties or early forties. All she saw was a smooth-faced, handsome man with polite, gentle manners, deep in sleep and dreaming.

The smile on his face was such that she decided not to interrupt him, envying him the sweetness of pleasant, loving dreams. He looked so content.

* * *

Others did not sleep as Yoshi flew over the broad expanses of the dry lands bearing only a few thin patches of green where man attempted to scratch an existence out of the poor soil.

Tommy was waiting for his flight to Cairo, then nonstop to Bangkok. Rossen had made an earlier connection to Manila, then a connection to Thailand. Tommy would arrive a short time before him.

Tommy wondered about Yoshi and why he had become what he was. True, they both killed. But Tommy knew with Yoshi it was not the same.

Even as children, Yoshi had a feeling to him. He always had to go to the extreme in everything. There was never any middle ground. He was always right. He had to win every game they played.

If Tommy won, Yoshi would sometimes sulk for days before his natural exuberance made him forgive his cousin and they would once more begin their games. But they never played at the regular children's games like hide-and-seek. Oh, they had their version. Seek-and-kill.

Usually, Tommy did not try as hard as Yoshi. He knew that Yoshi was better than him in most things. He had such incredible concentration when he chose to apply it. The martial arts, Shotokan, judo, different variations of kung fu: In these disciplines he would lose himself for hours on end, blocking out everything and everybody. When he had a katana in his hand, his teachers became very worried, for the blade seemed to be part of him, to come alive and, as with the legend of the cursed swords of the Muramasa, needing to drink blood.

Tommy had been more interested in life than death, but Yoshi was always talking about death in the strangest terms, almost affectionately. Tommy often thought that if he had been of the right age during the war, Yoshi would have been the first to volunteer to become kamikaze.

To Yoshi it would have been the ultimate experience. To fly high above the blue seas with the beasts of the air, to search out his prey on the waters thousands of feet beneath him. Then seeing it: Turn his machine, point its nose down, and dive, dive, dive, letting nothing stop him from reaching the object of his desire. To hear the wind scream as it passed over his wings, his heart beating ever faster as adrenaline pumped through his veins, feeding him.

Then, having overcome all obstacles, enemy fighters, antiaircraft fire, he would, in a last thrust of glory, immolate himself and his machine in a tremendous funeral pyre and in the doing destroy hundreds, possibly even thousands, of his Emperor's enemies.

Such a death would not be at all unwelcome for one such as he. That was the key to what he was doing now. He had grown up and had no one to play with. He had made up his own game, and the game, as always, had to be played out to the extreme, for there was no other way to stop him, save death.

Tommy's flight was announced, and he picked up his one nylon flight bag, which contained nothing to disturb airport security, and moved out to the international flight gates. As he passed between the myriad of strangers coming and going for a thousand different reasons, he carried with him the face of Yoshi, his boyhood friend and only living relative. The face of the man he had to kill.

An airport security guard saw the intense expression on the Oriental's face and made a note to follow him when he checked through security. He would give a hand signal to see that this man's luggage was most carefully examined. He had the look of a man about to do something terrible.

SIXTEEN

CHERNY LAY THE FOLDERS BACK ON HIS DESK. FOR weeks his people had been running computer comparisons, breaking down all the known information about each killing, reducing them and comparing them with all persons known and unknown who indulged in wet work in either government or private sector operations.

The first bit of correlated luck came through concerning the strange puncture mark found on the collarbone of the man in Los Angeles. One other killing had some of the same indicators. The back of a man's skull had been ripped off. The patch of skull torn away had the same kind of puncture in it. Most peculiar. Now, what could do that? And why use it one time to kill and another not to?

It was puzzling in the extreme. He had witnessed, he thought, nearly every kind of execution possible, but this was something new. It excited him. A mystery. He did enjoy mystery novels. Especially spy stories.

Outside the consulate, the heat beat at the windows and was forced back by the constant droning of an air conditioner, an American-made air conditioner, for which he was thankful. Those few manufactured in the Soviet Union never seemed to function very well.

Bangkok was sweltering. He enjoyed the vibrancy and mystery of the city, but detested the climate. In addition, he was somewhat weary. Jet lag, you know. Once he persuaded the chairman and Qaddafi to do as he suggested, even to the point of destination, he had immediately flown here. He wanted to be waiting in advance of both parties, the Palestinians and the hunters.

Waiting for him when he arrived was this pile of folders and photos. The computer-analysis people had made only a few correlations.

Crossing the room over a priceless carpet from Astrakhan, he went to the blackboard he had ordered when the first packet of data had come in. On it he began to try to put a picture together.

Item number one: The assassins were first-rate marksmen. That shot in Mexico had really been incredible.

Second: They were highly skilled and knew demolitions, hand-to-hand combat, and used at least two rather odd weapons—a blade with a chisel-shaped tip and the other, what?

The questions ate at him. Whoever they were, they left precious little to work with. There were any number of technicians with the same skills out there. He could name at least eight offhand. But they were not the ones. He had run a check on the three who did not work under the control of his office. Each was cleared of any participation.

That left the unknown again. But they were there. And they were coming to him. He had to be ready. They must be identified. Ah, it was giving him a migraine to be this close, and he still might lose them if they couldn't be spotted in time. He had only hours remaining to prepare a reception. But for whom?

Standing at the window, he saw a beggar across the street, one leg folded under him, the other stuck out on the sidewalk so the passers-by could see the sores on it. One hand was extended in whining supplication, holding what looked to be a brass bowl. There was no other hand, only a wrinkled stump, beckoning to the passersby to drop their change into the bowl.

Cherny turned away in disgust. Beggars were a blight, they should be stamped out. He knew that many of them created their own sores and wounds. At their hovels, they would pick at their flesh till it was raw, then smear feces over the fresh openings. He hoped the tetanus rate was 100 percent for them.

If there was one positive thing socialism had accomplished in Russia, it was that the beggars were gone from the streets. There, the slacker would have been made to work. The state would have given him a prosthetic hand, or at the very least a pirate's hook.

Hook! A hook was what could have made the strange puncture wounds! It began to come together. He needed verification, but at least now he had one thing to go on, something he could watch for. Stepping quickly to the desk, he called for the KGB section chief for Bangkok to come to him.

It took five minutes before Lieutenant Colonel Leonel Makrov knocked on his door. During that time, Cherny ran things back through his mind. There was a trick of letting the mind drift with a loose objective. In this manner it could scan all information in his subconscious and stop when something clicked. He carried his own computer with him.

A hook! There was something he recalled. It had also taken place in this area of the world a couple of years back. Something about an attempted rescue of American POWs still being held in Laos or Cambodia. He couldn't recall exactly which one it was.

But there had been information received that two Americans had gone in. And when they came out they were spotted at a border village and their presence reported as a matter of form. They had been alone, bringing no one out with them. In addition, they had been met later by a Thai intelligence official. But the item of extreme interest was that one of them had a hook for a hand.

"Come in, Comrade Makrov. Will you take tea?"

"No, thank you, comrade. I have already breakfasted in the commissary."

Cherny sat back, holding his fingers tip to tip under his chin. Makrov had a long history of service. Not one with a great deal of imagination, but once he was put on something he pursued it to the very end. Not unlike a bulldog, which he resembled somewhat. A peasant's broad, flat face, the thickening of the jowls. Tree-stump neck set on a barrel of a body. Odd that one with such a physical appearance would have a preference for teenage boys. But then, we all have our quirks.

"Comrade Makrov, you know that my authority is from the Directorate itself, do you not?"

The tree stump moved forward a bit, inclining the head a fraction to acknowledge that it did know.

"Very good. Then I have a job which is most sensitive and may prove to be even more violent."

Makrov's eyes began to get a touch of a spark to them. Another quirk of his nature was a passion for pain in whatever form it might be applied.

"Yes, comrade. What is it that I may do for you?"

Leaning over to emphasize the importance of his words, Cherny said, "First, I want this country covered. Every port of entry. Every hotel. Put everyone you can out on this. There will be at least two men coming in. Probably separately. One of them will have a hand which has been amputated. He may be wearing a hook in its place, or possibly a prosthetic device. Have your people make note of anyone bearing this description and also of anyone who is wearing gloves. Our target might conceal the hand."

Which to Cherny's thinking would be an act of incredible stupidity. Who in the tropics wore gloves? But one never knew. The target might be a bit self-conscious about his deformity and wish to conceal it. It was not unheard-of for a small vanity to destroy a man.

"You said there were at least two men, comrade. Is there no further description you can give me of them? Or any place to which they might go?"

Cherny shook his sculptured head slowly from side to side as he lit up a Winston, offering one to Makrov, which the Colonel declined. Smoking was a filthy habit.

"Believe me, Colonel, it is with deepest regret that I have no further data on these men.

But they are dangerous and they are smart. Take all precautions and do not have any of your people attempt to detain them or interfere with their movements in any manner. That would be a great mistake, and possibly cost us a successful mission."

Makrov nodded in agreement. "Very good, comrade. We shall observe and report any contact immediately to you. Is there anything else?"

Cherny stood and went back to the window. The beggar still begged for alms in the street.

"Yes, there is one more thing. A few years ago, there was an attempted rescue of American POWs supposedly still held in Cambodia or Laos. Two Americans went on that mission. They did not return with anyone. But if I recall correctly, they did play havoc while they were there. I wish for you to find me the report on that incident and bring it to me as soon as possible. We might have more information on our expected arrivals in the report. One of the would-be rescuers was a man with one hand. And I have never believed in too great an incidence of coincidence." (He liked that phrase, "incidence of coincidence.")

Turning back to face Makrov, he saw that he was scanning his blackboard, which he had planned for him to do anyway. "If you will, Comrade Colonel. We have so little time left. Our guests may be coming to us in a matter of hours."

Makrov understood he was being dismissed. He rose heavily from the chair. There was something about Cherny he liked. This was a cool one. He looked a bit of a fop. But there was steel behind the fine tailored Western clothes. No, he was not a cool one. He was cold. Cold as the steppes of Mother Russia in winter. And as dangerous.

Before he could close the door behind him, Cherny said softly, "Comrade, this is to be strictly between ourselves. No one else is to know anything about the operation. I have already arranged for some help from the outside to come to us. This is not to slight your abilities, or those of your staff. But these men have not worked in the area before and are less likely to be spotted by the opposition."

Makrov clicked his heels slightly in acceptance of the logic. "As you wish, comrade. I shall return instantly with the file you requested."

"Ah, by the way, Comrade Makrov: Do not sign this file out. I wish no record of it being brought to me."

Makrov hesitated a moment. This was irregular. But he had no choice. Theodorovich Cherny was not one to have as an enemy. He said only, "As I said earlier, comrade, as you wish."

SEVENTEEN

As the aircraft carrying Yoshi, Ibn-karim, Safar, Salmeh, and al-Hakim was lifting out of the pattern from New Delhi for Bangkok, Makrov returned with the data Cherny had requested. Placing the file on the desk in front of Cherny, he waited.

"Please sit down, comrade," Cherny invited, his eyes already reading the first page, "this should not take long. I do believe that we have found that which we sought. We have a partial description and even a name of sorts for one of them."

Makrov did not tell Cherny that he had read the file before bringing it to his hands. Bobbing his heavy head up and down in the manner of an overfed gorilla, he said, "That is very good to hear, comrade. Can you tell me what it is, so that I may transmit the descriptions to my men?"

Cherny played the game with Makrov. He knew without doubt that he had read the file first. He would have, too, if their positions had been reversed.

"Certainly, my friend." He used the phrase to let Makrov know his importance to him and the operation. "First, if I may think out loud: Ofttimes it helps to verbalize thoughts. Then I would welcome your observations and suggestions." *As if this Neanderthal would have anything of value to contribute except a more painful way of ending one's existence.*

"I now know better who we are going against. Two men, both Americans, one of them of Japanese descent. That is what threw me. The Japanese has only one hand. For the other he uses a hook, though I suspect he has some other interesting attachments for it as well, in particular an oddly shaped knife. You know how the Japanese were about creating things to kill and maim. They were an incredibly inventive people in this area."

While Makrov was gone, Cherny had made excellent use of the library. There he had found a book released by the Japanese Ministry of Culture on ancient arms and armor of Japan. In that book he found the chisel-tipped weapon: the *nambam-bo*. Peculiar name for anything, sounded like a bowl of bamboo soup.

"From the report our agents gave when these two came back across the border, they were

met by an official of the Thai government, as I
stated earlier. He obviously knew these men
quite well. Our agent there at the border village
unfortunately did not speak English. The only
word he could recall with any clarity was
'Shooter.' That is, I believe, what the Americans sometimes called their snipers during the
war, is it not, comrade?"

Makrov agreed with him instantly, though he
did not have the faintest idea of whether it was
true or not. He did not come to Southeast Asia
till after the war. "Yes, of course, comrade. You
are correct."

Cherny smiled his appreciation for Makrov's
specious reinforcement of his opinion.

"Yes. Now, as to the descriptions. The agent
said the Japanese was of slightly larger height
and frame than most of his countrymen. I
suspect this is due to the famous American
diet. The one called Shooter is a bit over six
feet, thin, with light hair and blue or grayish
eyes.

"That is not much, but it is a beginning.
Sooner or later the two will have to come
together. If they are missed when they come
into the country, we will be able to spot them
once they begin to move. There are only so
many roads in and out of Bangkok and I think I
know how to make them take the ones I want
them to."

Cherny rose. "Now if you will, Colonel, distribute this information to your men. I will continue to work and see if I cannot find out a bit more about these men. I have somewhere to start.

"But remember, as I said before, not a word of our purpose to anyone. All your men need to do is watch for two men with these characteristics. Especially have them pay close attention to anyone who is traveling alone. I do not believe that they would have had time to arrange the cover of traveling with a group."

Makrov left, several questions filtering through his mind. This thing Cherny had for the two assassins was not dedication to the principles of the greater Soviet, or the continuing struggle of the proletariat against the capitalists. Not at all. There was something personal here. Cherny wanted them as a man wants sex. It was in his voice and the slight trembling manner of his body when he spoke of them, not as enemies of the party, but as one would of a lover he has not seen for a long time. Cherny *lusted* after them.

The idea excited Makrov a bit. He would arrange for his new lover to spend a bit of time with him later this evening. The boy was delightful. Sixteen, and he had been a virgin when Makrov took him the first time. But he learned so fast and was so very eager to please. He would buy something nice for him later. Now he had to get on with Comrade Cherny's plans. He did have to confess to a bit of curiosity himself about the two Americans who were coming in. Cherny seemed to be absolutely certain they were coming. How did he know?

As soon as Makrov was gone, Cherny went to the basement of the consulate where the communications section monitored the airwaves and received their own instructions from Moscow. It was also the computer center.

The officer in charge of the day shift was a thin Georgian with an obvious overbite and bad breath. Cherny instructed him as he handed over a single page of data.

"I wish to see all correlations which can be found pertaining to two men with these characteristics. They are Americans, one of Japanese descent. The other one, the Caucasian, is called Shooter. I would suspect that during the Vietnam debacle they were in the American armed forces and employed as snipers.

"Go to Moscow Central if you have to. Get into the mainframe and find them for me as soon as possible. Time is of the essence. This has the highest priority."

In Moscow, the electronic request was fed into the computer which rested in the basement of KGB headquarters on Dzherinsky Street. Tapes spun, disks whirred, chips heated up, and circuits opened to scroll onto the CRT all information fed into it by their sources in

Southeast Asia, the Middle East, Central and South America.

And even some tidbits from some of their agents in the American government. The machine searched through millions of bits of data, then began to form green phosphor letters on the screen. This was then broken down into a coded signal which was fed back to the communications center in Bangkok. The process, once the computer had the key elements to cross-reference, took less than fifteen minutes.

As soon as the data came in, the Georgian technician signaled upstairs for Cherny, who came himself to receive the hard copy.

"Thank you for your efficient and rapid service, comrade." He bent over to look at the man's identity tag. "Ah, yes, Comrade Vasili. I will make note of your efficiency in my report."

He left the skinny Georgian with his bony chest swelling out with pride. He had been addressed by his first name.

Once more alone, Theodorovich Cherny digested the information he'd received from Moscow Central. There was not a great deal of it, but what he found was most interesting.

These two men had been very active. They had not been connected with the current difficulties, because they never seemed to have any government attachment of any sort. Always they seemed to be working for themselves.

Were they still doing just that? Could they be turned? He thought not. They were—he smiled—like the romantics of fiction, Don Quixotes jousting with windmills.

But they had been around since the end of the war. Africa, Nicaragua, Laos, and now it was believed that they were living in Central America. No exact location known. Which was unfortunate, but to be expected. They were not on a security watch list.

As far as Moscow was concerned, they were only common mercenaries of little value, though it had been confirmed they had been involved with an operation against the Sandinistas which proved quite costly to the fledgling regime. But they were used only as common hired guns. Nothing more.

However, for Theodorovich Cherny, what he had was more than enough. He had names and he had pictures, sent by telefax at the same time as the computer readout, taken of them when they were in Costa Rica. Not the best photographs in the world, but good enough to reduce the chance of error if they were spotted coming in. These he would have sent immediately to Colonel Makrov.

Cherny read over the data once more before it hit him like a blow between the eyes: the names! Rossen the Shooter, and the Japanese-American, Tomanaga.

Could it be? He did not put much faith in the

laws of coincidence. Tomanaga! Well, well. This just might prove to be even more entertaining than he had expected. Whatever the truth was, when they came into Bangkok, he would know it.

EIGHTEEN

TOMMY KNEW THEY WERE GETTING CLOSER. Yoshi was running for home. No, running wasn't the right word. Yoshi was going home. If they missed him here, the next stop would be Japan.

When he came in, there was also a JAL landing from Tokyo. Tommy tried to blend in with the horde of Japanese businessmen and tourists as they passed through customs and immigration, hoping that one more Japanese would not be noticeable.

Rossen was coming in from Manila a bit later, about six. Tommy went ahead to the hotel they had agreed on and was about to check in with the number Mr. Smith had given them. Before he could set his bags down and take a leak, the phone in his Silom Plaza room rang.

The voice was by now easily recognizable. He gave Tommy the location of a drop near the hotel. It took Tommy only a few minutes to cover the distance to the stationery store where a purchase had been made in his name. The woman behind the counter asked only to see his passport to make certain he was the one intended for the order. She thanked him, went into a rear room, and came out less than a minute later with a packet wrapped in bright flower-print paper. "This is for you, sir."

Tomanaga paid a 420-baht bill and returned to his room. In the packet was what current data they had on Yoshi and the terrorists. He kept separating his cousin from the Arabs.

They were definitely in-country. Also on the deck, having come in the day before them, were two KGB types who normally spent most of their time in the Middle East. There were two photographs each of the new arrivals to the game. The shots had obviously been taken when the two men cleared customs and were leaving the terminal in Bangkok. Tommy wondered whether anyone had taken his.

The enclosed note suggested caution. This could be some professional help coming in to nail his and Rossen's hides to the wall.

It was nearly time. He left the hotel, taking a three-wheel motorcycle taxi the mile and a half down Silom Road to the Patpong red-light district. He had the driver make a couple of turns to throw off any tails. A tail would have trouble in the congested traffic mix of motorcycles, buses, cars, and the occasional water buffalo being driven through a herd of saffron-robed monks and other pedestrians. But if anyone was on him, Tommy didn't think they'd be able to stay with him after the second turn down a narrow one-way street. He would have spotted them.

If the plane was on time, Rossen should have cleared customs by now and be on his way into the city. Give him an hour to check in and get located, take a crap and a smoke, and he should be joining him in, say, two hours. That would give Tommy time to speak to Terry, the owner of the Tavvern on Patpong II.

Paying the driver, he got off at Patpong I and began walking through the narrow streets beneath myriad signs reading Go-Go Bar, Sex Show, and Massage. Patpong had changed greatly over the years. It was cleaner, and the hustlers didn't hit on you as heavily as they had years ago. Now they had a much bigger and more affluent selection of potential customers to pick from, instead of the crowd of U.S. airmen from the bases and GIs on leave from the war.

Going past the Steeplechase Bar, where Jimmy the Belgian still ran his show, he turned to the right, going the short half block to Patpong II. He turned left a few steps and he was there. The rest of the street was drowned in sound, each bar and cabaret competing for attention with stereos wide open. The Tavvern was an oasis in this two-block mini-asylum. It was a good place to stop, sit down with Terry, have a quiet beer, and wait.

Waiting was not something Rossen liked to do very much, unless he was on a kill site. But Tommy made a point of being a bit of a stoic; he never showed any impatience. To do so would be a lack of control, visible weakness. He would never permit that. All his life he had been careful never to give anyone an edge of any kind which could be used against him. He had to wait, and that was all there was for it. Besides which, there were times when his Oriental calm and basic cool would drive Rossen up the wall. Just that made it all worthwhile.

Soon the Shooter would make his appearance and join his partner. Of that there was no doubt. His people had the airports covered. He would come in by air. There was no other mode of travel fast enough for them to get here and be sure their quarry would still be in-country.

They would come by air and the international airport was completely covered, as were the secondary strips on the odd chance that someone might try to slip him in through one of the smaller fields. Anywhere a jet of any size could set down was covered.

He would know within minutes when the next one hit the ground. The Japanese was already spotted. They had picked him up at the airport. He had been lost when his motorcab made a turn in traffic, but no matter, they would pick him up again later.

Now, when the big one came, he would set the stage and have them all in his bag. A good thought. This would raise his credibility factor very high. New position and new powers.

As for Yoshi and the Palestinians, they were nothing. If they died, who cared? There were always plenty of fanatics in the world to take their place. For the time being he had them tucked away in a safe house. The Palestinians were enjoying the favors of some of the local ladies, but the Japanese stayed to himself. A stoic, Cherny thought.

Not good. People who keep too tight a rein on their emotions usually explode at inopportune times. He would keep an eye on him. A close eye. Especially now that another Tomanaga was coming to see him.

He had much to plan in advance: how to let the Japanese and his partner locate their targets without it being too obvious. He had to be very careful not to scare them off. The trap must always be set with great care. Which was exactly what he had done with the eager cooperation of Colonel Makrov. A Trojan horse of sorts, but it had worked before.

The important thing was for the opposition to believe they were doing it all. Of course, someone from one or more sources was keeping the killers up to date with current intelligence. That was what could be used against them. Let them feed the two assassins their information. They would believe it then.

He loved this game. Move and countermove. It had taken nearly all of one night to come up with a variation of an old gambit, to structure a scenario which the other agencies would pick up on and interpret in the manner he wished. One which, even if they found out the truth, they would still have to play.

Good God! It was humid. Bangkok in the summer was like living in a steam bath. Put on a fresh shirt and it was sopping wet in five minutes. He thought the greatest blessing of modern technology was the air conditioner. He didn't know how the early colonials survived year in and year out without it. Maybe it was because they didn't have any choice in the matter.

Not important. He'd had a bit of luck. His people working with the DEA had come up with something, something important. They had lost the terrorists when they hit country yesterday. Now they just might have a location on them. It seemed to fit.

A courier for the BLA, the Burmese Liberation Army, who were heavily involved with drug shipments out of the country, had been killed by a beer truck while crossing a street just two hours earlier. Just one of those never-to-be-planned-for accidents.

On his body was fifty thousand dollars, a Walther PPK pistol, and two letters. One was ostensibly a note from an importer questioning current prices and shipping costs of rice to Australia. The other was a personal letter to the general manager of a lumber company up near Chiang Mai.

The letter said that the extra help asked for would be showing up within three days and that the manager should show the sender's cousins all consideration until they were settled in properly.

All this would have meant little, and it was pretty thin. But the manager of the lumber company was a known PLO sympathizer, and a Palestinian to boot. The drug people also operated out of that area, and the other letter obviously had to do more with drugs than rice. The dope business was integral to the guerrilla movement. The money from drugs was used to help finance their operations.

Tie this in with the appearance of the KGB types who had shown up, both of whom had strong connections to the PLO. One of them was even now on his way north, probably to visit the guerrilla camp.

None of the data by itself meant very much, but when put together, it gave him a clue. Yoshi Tomanaga, Yousef Safar, and Hasan Salmeh were heading to the frontier. There they would be under the protection of the guerrillas in a remote area with little, if any, effective government presence. They would be very hard to get to if they made it that far.

From the letter it seemed as if they were going to make a stop at the lumber camp first. If that was the case, and Rossen and Tommy were there ahead of them, or at least got there before they pulled out for the frontier, they might have a chance to make their hits and get out.

Once the terrorists disappeared into the jungle, no one could tell when they might have a chance to nail them again.

A one-handed nisei and a six-foot-one, blue-eyed American bumming around through the jungles of Burma would, to say the least, be very noticeable.

Jones lit up a smoke, sucked the acrid fumes deep, then let it out slowly, blowing several small, tight rings. Luck! We have had a bit of incredible luck. Almost too good to be true, he thought, smiling as he took another drag, turning the tip of the cigarette bright red.

My dad used to say, "If something looks too good to be true, then it probably is." I think Comrade Cherny is trying to fuck with us. That's okay. As long as we know it. Now, if the name of the game is fuck your neighbor, we know how to play that, too." Jones ground out the butt.

This could get to be very, very entertaining. At any rate, we've got to bite. There isn't any other thing working at this point. Either this is a legitimate piece of good fortune or it's a setup. As long as we play it from the beginning like it is a setup, we should be able to pull it off.

NINETEEN

STEPPING INSIDE THE TAVVERN WAS NOT UNLIKE
going into the Europa in Gaute. Terry was the
English version of Freddie. Over twenty years
in the tropics, he looked his part: a retired Brit
sergeant major, with square shoulders and
face, calm, bright, brown eyes, and military
mustache.

He was the man up front, but his wife, who
was the largest Oriental woman Tommy had
ever seen, was the real muscle. She wasn't fat;
she was well proportioned and very feminine
all the way from top to bottom. She was just big
and tough, the way only a woman who has lived
hard and seen much in a short life can be.
Nobody got away with shit around her.

She was content to do most of the hard work
and let Terry handle public relations, which
meant doing a few side deals from time to
time, taking care of his friends' problems, and

offering solutions to the world at large, which, as with Freddie (and to his extreme disgust), were never acted upon.

Terry came out from his normal place of operation at the right end of the bar, where he pored over the two English-language newspapers published each day.

"Hey there, Tommy, good to see you again, mate. Where's your buddy? Not far away, I'll wager, what?"

He called to his wife, who gave Tommy a bear hug of affection, set him up a Sangson, made a couple of lewd suggestions about the different applications possible for him and his hook, and left. She had urgent business in the back or she would have hung around a bit longer. Her fortune-teller was in to read the cards for her. There was little which she would let interfere with that.

Terry just smiled benevolently. "It's her way, mate. And who's to say she's wrong? She's done quite all right listening to that old dyke witch. Like Shakespeare said, 'more things on heaven and earth, Horatio.' Or was it George? Never the mind. You know what I mean."

Tommy caught a glimpse of a small woman wearing jeans, a man's plaid shirt with rolled-up sleeves, and a short butch haircut over a wizened, shriveled face which could make one believe in the unknown.

The only other customer was a Canadian, in to see if he could find a deal on some hardwood furniture for his furniture shop in Montreal. He was much more interested in the girls who passed by the window than in the one-handed Japanese and retired British sergeant.

"Is your friend coming in later?"

Tommy nodded. "Should show up in an hour or so. But I wanted to talk to you first. We have a bit of work to do in the area and might need a few things, and possibly some people. So I just wanted to touch bases with you first, to let you know."

"Sure, Tommy. Just let me know what and how many of whatever it is and I'll dig it up for you somewhere."

Tommy had a sudden hot flash run over his body. Just a second; then it was gone.

Yoshi sat up straight. He had been dreaming. Someone or something was very close to him. Coming for him. In his sleep he knew only that whatever it was, was right. It should be. The dream was not a nightmare. Yoshi never had them. Nightmares were for those with weak minds and childish consciences. He did believe that at times, when the mind was at rest, it opened up to many outside influences unseen by light of day. There was no doubt in his mind that whatever he had experienced in his sleep was true. Something was coming for him.

Lying back down, he looked through a rattan blind at the brightness which was turning to red-gold dusk outside. Soon he would be going home. Back to Japan. That, too, was a feeling which had touched him in his sleep.

It would be good to return home. To the past. There was nothing in the future of any value. Only in the past did one find honor and truth as in the path of Geba, the way of Divine Violence.

Closing his eyes, Yoshi prepared to go back to sleep. Perhaps the dream would come again and be clearer. He hoped so, for there was little in this world which gave him pleasure.

Sleep was not to be, nor pleasant dreams. A voice at his door shattered whatever hope he had of recapturing his mystery. Hasan yelled through the shutters, "It's time to go. We are going north."

So, Yoshi thought, *you have at last managed to drag yourself away from the women*. Feeling drained by what he thought would be more dreary time spent with cretinous maniacs, Yoshi swore that this was his last move.

He was too close to home to change directions. He would go with them one last time. Something, his dream perhaps, made him feel that it was the thing to do for now. He would go with them to the mountains. Then he would return home.

Rossen was on the deck, tired, wondering how one can feel so dirty when he had done nothing but sit on his ass for twenty or so hours in a very clean aircraft. His legs ached from sitting in too-small seats. He had the money to go first-class but people there liked to visit and talk too much. In the rear of the aircraft, he had had a turbaned, spade-bearded Sikh beside him who spoke no English. He certainly didn't speak any Hindi, or whatever it was they spoke. It was peaceful.

Going straight through the Nothing to Declare line, Rossen was given a quick look but, as he was only carrying hand luggage consisting of one flight bag and a nylon suitcase, the official, who was more interested in a young blond girl from Norway, stamped his papers, and he was through to the outside.

Picking up a taxi at the desk provided for such services, he headed on into the main city, telling the driver to take him to the Malaysia Hotel off Rama IV Road. It had seen better days, but it was still close to the center of things and the food wasn't bad.

Heading in, he was as always amazed at the contrast of the country. Golden-domed wats and temples competed with billboards for Mercedes and Toyota, modern high rises and thatched peasants' houses alongside of rice paddies.

A truckload of Thai troops passed him, turning off to the left where an army installation of some sort was established. Probably for airport security. There had been nearly twenty coups in the last twenty years.

But it didn't seem to keep the tourists away. They still came in droves: men to search through the fleshpots of the Orient for willing, golden-skinned girls in whose soft arms they perhaps recaptured a bit of fantasy about another younger time, others to buy the drugs coming down in a flood from the Golden Triangle. Hippies, students, Euro-scum in search of mind-expanding experiences. Leftover mercs and lost soldiers who couldn't go home anymore. Peace Corps do-gooders and industrialists.

Thailand was booming as never before. It attracted everyone. There was something here for all. For him, too. He hoped this would be the last of it. If "Smith" was on the money, they might be able to end it all here.

He wanted to go back home. This kind of killing was not what he liked to do. It was too much like being no more than a hired assassin, without reason or morals. Just a killer, no more. And there was Tommy. The thing with his cousin was eating at him bad. What was going to happen when they finally met? Would he be able to cut it and take—what did he say his name was?—Yoshi? Yeah, would he be able to take Yoshi down? If Tommy didn't, then by God he would. Even if it did piss Tommy and whatever Asiatic honor-code shit was on his mind. He wasn't going to let Tommy fall, even if it meant they had to break up the partnership.

Checking back over his shoulder, Rossen tried to see if he could spot anyone on his tail.

He wasn't very good at it and knew that if they were laying for him, he probably wouldn't be able to shake them till he got into town. No matter. He and Tommy would move out as soon as they met over at the Tavvern. They would leave their things in the hotels in case they were located and pick up what they needed as they went. So if he could drop off any tail between the hotel and the Tavvern, they should be all right for time. Mr. Smith would take care of their special requirements.

They were into town. Samlors, the brightly decorated, three-wheeled taxis, darted in and out of traffic like mechanical butterflies. He'd take two or three before heading over to the Patpong area. No one could keep up with one, especially if you gave the driver an extra forty baht to go the wrong way on a one-way street for a block or two. Anyone in a car would be stopped and another samlor or motorcycle would be easy to spot.

He *was* picked up. A photo of him was in Cherny's hands within an hour after he had cleared customs. He was not the only one. Makrov's people were taking shots of everyone who remotely resembled the description of their target. The flight they came in on was noted, and men were assigned to follow the most promising suspects. When it was broken down, it did not require more men than Makrov was able to supply. To find one middle-aged, thin American with light hair and blue or gray eyes, who was traveling alone, narrowed things considerably.

There were two others on Rossen's flight who were close to his general description, but even with the less-than-perfect copies of the telefax photo, the watchers could be certain that neither was the one they were after. And of the three, Rossen was the only one who had traveled alone.

The tail stayed with him, working in relays, until he was deposited at his hotel. Within an hour he had left the hotel wearing jeans and khaki short-sleeved shirt, and carrying a gray windbreaker. Over his shoulder was a small flight bag. Then, as with the Japanese, he was lost in traffic when he took a samlor rather than a car.

All this served only to whet Cherny's appetite. He complimented Makrov lavishly for his excellent work. "Don't concern yourself, comrade. When they return to their hotels we will pick them up again. In the meantime, our other guests will soon be on their way to the lumber camp. From there they will be moved to the guerrilla camp within a few days."

Cherny had no intention of moving the terrorists. That might make it too difficult for the Shooter and the Japanese to reach them. No. Everything would take place at the lumber camp. And he and his men would be there to make certain that all went in orderly fashion.

Yoshi, Hasan, Yousef, and the rest were only
bait.

With a bit of luck, this whole game could be
over within forty-eight hours. He knew his
Trojan horse had been covered. Now it was
only a time to wait, to be patient just a bit
longer.

"Comrade Colonel, I believe it is time for us
to prepare the reception for the Americans.
With the two men I have at my disposal and, I
think, two more of yours. That will be more
than sufficient to handle things if the assassins
try to kill our friends while en route from the
lumber camp to the guerrilla base. I will take
charge of the security detail myself."

TWENTY

MAKROV WAS NOT SO CERTAIN THAT CHERNY WOULD have it all his own way. He had one thing Cherny did not. True, the comrade was sophisticated, intelligent, and well-dressed. He was capable of subtleties beyond Makrov's limitations. But Makrov knew his own limitations.

Cherny was a killer, but of a more refined sort. Makrov had read the reports concerning the wave of terror directed against the Palestinians and their supporters. These two men probably were not nearly as sophisticated as the debonair Soviet.

Cherny acted as if he wanted to make a game of it. These men he was after would kill instantly, without hesitation or conversation, giving Cherny no opportunity to impress them with his genius.

He, Colonel Leonel Makrov, had survived while many more intelligent men had killed themselves playing games. He had the distinct feeling that he would still be around long after Comrade Cherny had his well-dressed ass blown away. That was an American phrase he liked: *blown away*. Very descriptive.

However, if Cherny wished to handle things in this manner, he would assist him in every way permitted and, as usual, report everything to Moscow Central. There was the very faint hope that they might permit him to remove Cherny. It was, as he knew, only wishful thinking. But then, one can always dream, can't one?

A shadow passed over him before the figure was reflected in the mirror behind the bar.

"Hey, Jim. Glad you made it." Shaking hands with Terry, he sat down beside Tommy and ordered a beer from the girl behind the bar, taking her away from what seemed to be an almost religious devotion to her fingernails . . . which she went back to polishing and buffing after she had filled his order.

"How was the flight?" Tommy asked.

"Probably the same as yours, boring and long. You talk to Terry about anything yet?"

"Not really. I was waiting for you to come in. Our Mr. Smith has passed on some information. It looks like everything we want is in the country. I'll fill you in on details later. Nothing too urgent right now. We'll give Mr. Smith another call later, okay?"

"Okay."

Other customers began to come in, half filling the bar, refugees from the increasing crescendo of noise on the streets outside. It was getting dark. The lights were coming on. Patpong was coming alive for another night. The streets were getting crowded with buyers and sellers of whatever one wanted to satisfy his fantasies. The sellers wanted the money. The buyer, dreams.

Most of Terry's customers were regulars, the expatriates who, for a thousand different reasons, or possibly none, lived outside of whatever their mother country might be. He had no trouble in his bar and didn't permit any, other than the few isolated disturbances which any tavern keeper has to expect now and again. Most of these were handled by his wife.

There is something incredibly impressive about a six-foot two-inch Asian woman with a temper. She could back off nearly anyone. Tough sailors and veteran marines, Green Berets and British commandos had all backed away from her temper, and done so without shame.

The Chinese tactician Sun Tsu had said in his writings, "There are some bridges not to cross and some battles not to fight." Terry normally just twisted his mustache and smiled sweetly, tolerantly, as if the poor benighted chaps who started trouble were only simpleminded children and not at all dangerous.

Getting up from his stool at the corner, Terry said to Rossen and Tommy, "Look, I know you blokes want to chat a bit. I'll just go get meself a bowl of noodles outside while you talk."

Rossen answered for them. "Right, Terry. Sorry to be so short. But I'm a little bushed. Let us get a few things settled and we'll talk later, all right?"

"Certainly." With that, Terry folded his paper neatly, slapped it under his right arm as if it were a sergeant major's swagger stick, and purposefully marched outside for another confrontation with the spicy, chili-laden food of Thailand.

Rossen and Tommy moved over to a table in the corner farthest from the door, where they could talk.

The girl questioned them without speaking as to whether they wanted another beer. Seeing that they did not, she returned her attention to her cuticles and life continued.

"Okay, Tommy, what do you have?"

"Our people are definitely here, and Smith thinks we may have acquired some unwelcome company. Some Ivans have shown up, maybe KGB types. So he wants us to watch our collective asses. I'll give him a call in a few minutes and see if there's any update. But I think things are going to move fast from here on out."

"God, I hope so. I'm starting to wish Green had just left us out of this and used someone else. I'd like to get this shit over with and go home. I still think we're getting too old for this kind of life. Why can't we do like Terry? Open a nice saloon, have a few good girls working, and take it easy."

Tommy signaled for a round of beers and received a totally disinterested look from the bartender, who reluctantly placed the cap back on a bottle of nail luster, then, careful not to let the damp beer bottles touch her inch-long nails, carried the beer over to them as if she were transporting a cargo of live plague bacteria.

When she had returned to what was by now obviously her main and driving concern in life, Tommy answered Rossen's last question.

"We tried that once in Guate, remember? A hundred thousand dollars down the fucking tube. We are not businessmen. The only chance we have is to give our money to someone else and let them take care of it and us, with the knowledge that if they fuck up, we fuck them up."

"Yeah, I guess you're right. Forget it. Hang in here, I'll give Smith a call." Going into the back, Rossen passed Terry's wife and her fortune-teller. She was so involved with the cards, she never noticed him.

"We've been waiting," the voice on the other end of the line said curtly.

Rossen was not in a good mood. "Who gives a fuck if you've been waiting or not? We got problems of our own. So knock that shit off and give me a readout. What's going down?"

The voice hesitated; it wanted to respond in terse military terms, but wisely understood that that would not impress this man.

"Never mind. At this time, because of the information and other items of importance, I think we had better meet face-to-face. After all, this could be the last stop if we play it right."

Rossen didn't know just what was meant, but he had been curious about the voice on the phone since the beginning. And there were some things that you had to sit down at the table to clear up.

"All right, when and where, Mr. Smith?"

"Take a samlor and go to the Hualompong Railway Station. Across from the Thai Song Creet Hotel is a Chinese restaurant with a green dragon painted on the window. Meet me there in one hour. Don't worry about spotting me. I know you. I'll give you the name of our mutual friend for ID. Okay?"

Rossen grimaced. *And I thought the spooks only came out Halloween.* "Of course, secret agent, sir. We shall follow instructions to the letter. I shall be carrying a copy of the London *Times.* Two weeks out of date, opened to the funny pages."

The line went dead. Rossen grinned, knowing the comments being vocalized at the other end of the now dead phone.

Terry had come back in while he was gone.

"Well, you chaps getting things sorted out, are you?"

"Yeah, Terry. We'll know more in an hour or two. C'mon, Tommy, we got a meet. Terry, just keep our bar tab running, will you?"

Terry twisted his mustache with practiced fingers. "Of course, I will. I've been keeping it running since you were last here. That's about two years now, what?"

Tommy groaned. "You mean we ran out on a tab and we have a bar bill here for two years?"

Terry smiled. "Not to worry. Your credit's good. At least it is until my wife finds out. Then I think you had better look for some quite stout interest charges. Part of which may include some major portions of your anatomy.

"But then, as I said, not to worry. Old Terr is here to take care of all of you lost waifs in the tropics. Now, get on with you. And ring me up if you need anything."

TWENTY-ONE

BANGKOK CHANGED WITH THE PASSING OF THE heat of the day: the streets freshened by the dusk rains, moths flying around streetlights and the fires from stands selling food; then, from the dark, would come a faster, more determined blackness, which swept down on the moths with thin, shrill squeaks of conquest, then the bat would take one of the mindless creatures off to feed on it in the night.

The streets were lined with stalls of food from the valleys and mountains—melons, mangoes, papaya, and plantain. The energy level of the city picked up with the dark. So did the violence. There were still areas where strangers did not go alone or uninvited. There were colonies of Chinese, Cambodians, and Vietnamese, Malays and Indians. All kept to themselves inside their enclaves. There were unwritten signs posted: If you are not one of us, do not enter.

Their samlor whipped in and out of the frantic traffic, squeezing between buses and trucks with only inches to spare, the rail-thin, pock-faced driver never once looking back.

Tommy said nothing. Rossen knew he was thinking of what was to come when he met his cousin. He wished he could help, but he didn't know the right words . . . if there were any.

The rat-faced driver of the gaudy red and sequined samlor deposited them three blocks from the rail station. They would walk the rest of the way. Getting off, Rossen asked, *"Tao ry?"*

Sixty baht. He didn't feel like haggling and left the driver thinking to himself how stupid foreigners were as he puttered off into the night.

When they came near the station, Tommy hung back in a doorway to see if he could pick up on any tail. Rossen went on ahead, going into the Thai Song Creet Hotel lobby first, then waiting for Tommy to move before crossing the street to follow him into the restaurant named, appropriately enough, the Emerald Dragon.

A diminutive Chinese girl with thin slits for eyes and round cheeks with a touch of rose painted on them, met them at the door. The face wasn't great, but the slit in her dark blue satin cheongsam showed a very graceful length of calf and thigh.

"Are you looking for Mr. Smith, sirs?"

Rossen nodded, and she led them to the rear, to a cubicle which had a sliding door behind which the customers could dine in privacy. It was still early for the dinner rush and there were only a few people at the tables. All looked to be Chinese; Rossen thought the food must be good here.

She slid the door open to their cubicle, where embroidered walls depicted cranes in flight over tall jagged peaks. For the first and, Rossen hoped, the last time, they met face-to-face with Mr. Smith.

Jones did not rise, merely indicated for them to enter and sit on the opposite side of the table, where they would be eye-to-eye. In quick, clipped Cantonese he ordered tea. The girl bowed her head and left to fill his order. No one said anything until she returned, poured the steaming *cha*, and left them, closing the screen behind her.

"Well, Mr. Rossen and Mr. Tomanaga. I have wanted to meet you for some time and express my gratitude and admiration for the work you've been doing."

Tommy sipped on his *cha*, leaving the conversation, for the time being, to Rossen, who asked tersely, "What do you have for us, Mr. Smith?"

Leaning back, Jones smacked his lips appreciatively over the flavor of the black tea. "Well, gentlemen, it appears that we have our party spotted. They are going, if they are not there already, to a lumber camp run by a Palestinian in the highlands to the northeast of Chiang Mai near the Burmese border. If we are going to meet up with them, it had better be there, before they cross over the border to join ranks with some rather unpleasant people. As of right now, I have people already at the lumber camp to keep it under surveillance.

"We also have at least two KGB types here, who have in the past been strongly connected with the Palestinians, including the training of a number of the leaders of Black September. There may be others."

Rossen shook his head. "How does that change things?"

Jones leaned forward. "It doesn't, unless you say it does. I just wanted you to know. It may be a setup. Too many things have happened to bring us here to be coincidence. I think the Russkies are trying to get you to come to them."

He paused, refilling his thin lacquered cup with more steaming *cha*. "If this new element throws you off, I'll understand. You have done a hell of a job anyway. The PLO, PFFL, and Black September will never feel completely secure again."

Rossen bit back bitterly, *"You'll* understand! Who the fuck's asking you to understand anything! You think we went into this because we want you to understand? I don't give a shit about what you like or don't like. Me and

Tommy are in this for our own reasons, and they haven't got a goddamn thing to do with you, or whoever employs you. So take your understanding and stick it up your ass."

Jones started to snap back, then held off. They were right. He had been condescending, and that was not the way to handle them. "You're right. I just got stuck in my own job profile. You call the shots and tell me what you want and that's what I'll do. Okay?" He straightened up. "All right, sarge. You and your partner have it. Is there anything you especially want us to do or get for you, Mr. Tomanaga?"

Tommy put down his cup. He was finished with the *cha*, the conversation. "Just what my partner said, Mr. Smith. That will be sufficient for our needs."

Rossen got up, sliding the screen open, and looked out right to left. There was nobody within listening range. "Let's go, Tommy. We need to find a place to crash for the night."

Jones asked, "Do you want to stay at one of our safe houses? I can arrange that easy enough."

"No, thanks, we'd rather take our chances on the street."

Jones refused to be drawn into another bout of temper. "As you wish, gentlemen. If you will contact me in the morning, I'll give you an update on what's going down."

They left, leaving Jones alone, wondering if it would ever be possible to get men like these under control again. They had been out in the cold too long. They were mavericks. Still, sometimes the world needed a few men who didn't go by the rules and still did things their way, instead of blindly following formula and orders.

When they left the Emerald Dragon, Rossen was still a bit uptight. He felt he had nearly lost it back there. He should have had better control. Maybe it was jet lag. Whatever, he knew it was wrong to fly off the handle like that.

"Okay, Tommy, let's find someplace to lay it down for the night. I got to crash. What's the best way to go?"

Hotels required passports and identification, and were easy to watch. They did the next best thing, or possibly the best thing: called Terry, had him send a couple of girls to them, and checked into the Thai equivalent of a no-tell motel, a place where foreigners came and went without questions. A steam bath in the room, a round or two with the ladies, and both zombied out until dawn when, as did ladies of the night all over the world, the girls left for home.

TWENTY-TWO

IN THE MORNING THEY MADE CONTACT WITH JONES again at the same restaurant, and went over what he had.

"It's a go. The target is at the camp. Inside this envelope,"—he passed over a not bulky but substantial manila envelope—"are aerial photos of the region and the camp. A breakdown on personnel employed. The security profile and pictures of much of the camp and personnel including the Palestinian running things.

"Your people are being guarded in a small compound, half a click from the main sawmill. It's got wire and guards around it. So far, I only have a count of four full-time guards, rotating in eight, three-hour shifts. There might be some people we don't know about. In fact, I would count on it. The Ivans haven't shown up anywhere. That's a pretty good sign they're close to the camp.

"Parked outside is a Toyota van. Inside is the stuff you asked for last night, including a couple of lightweight armored vests and some other goodies you might want to put to use."

Jones waited for them to ask something, anything. Rossen said only, "If that's all you got, then I guess we'll be going."

"That's all there is. You don't want or need anything more?" Jones was surprised. He knew they were independent, but this was taking it a bit far.

"No. I think the time to do it is now. You agree, Tommy?"

Tommy nodded his head. He wanted to get it over with.

"Okay then, Mr. Smith. If it's okay with Tommy, then I guess it's okay with me. We go. We'll set up the rest of the show our own way. Just as before."

Jones smacked the table with his hand. "By God, I wish there was something more I could do for you."

Rossen locked eyes with him. "You can, Mr. Smith. At this point stay out of the way. Any new faces up there are liable to get some holes in them. We might not have the time to determine who is with us and who is against us. It's a lot easier if we can consider every face out there a hostile and legitimate target."

Jones understood what he meant. Stay out of

it. Or take his chances. "As you say, Mr. Rossen, as you say. You'll have a free-fire zone up there all to yourself."

"Good. Now, we don't have much time, so give me the keys to the van and we'll get on with what we have to do."

They left Jones sitting by himself, drinking his tea, looking as if he had all the time in the world to do nothing.

Cherny had moved up to the lumber camp. He and his men were the good guys. His own specialists from the Middle East section of the KGB were on site. He was in the compound with the terrorists; his men were outside the perimeter of the camp.

They were waiting. Waiting for the Shooter and his partner to show. To make a move. When they hit the compound, they would be trapped between his men on the outside and the Palestinians and himself on the inside. That gave them an advantage of seven against two. He had no doubt that the native guards posted to secure the compound would be easily eliminated by the hunters. That was all part of the plan. It would make the Americans confident. Then, when they moved against the house, he would have them.

The first stop was back at the Tavvern for a quick talk with Terry. He was at his usual place by the bar.

"Terry, we need a few things from you and we need them now. Time is important. But we can pay whatever the freight is."

Terry perked up. "Why, then, my boys, if money is not a problem, then very little else is either. Tell Uncle Terr all about it. I'm at your service always." He held his finger to his nose indicating a matter of confidence. "By the by, I think it would be a good idea for you to settle your bill before we go any further. My wife's been going through some of the back accounts. If it doesn't balance it could become a bit bloody around here. Know what I mean?"

They paid up, then told Terry what they needed. Transport. A pilot who knew the area they were going into and one that would stay where he was supposed to for the promised amount of time and bring them back.

"No problem, boys. I have a good man for you. An Australian. Does a bit of independent flying for several gents up that way. Knows it like the head of his organ. He'll know where to take you. Don't you worry about that. And he'll bring you back if you're able to make rendez-vous on time. If he doesn't wait as agreed, why, then, I'll kill him."

Terry said this with that British lilt to his voice which was as pleasant as talking about the flowers in one's garden and absolutely serious at the same time. He would do exactly as he said. Terry always guaranteed whomever he contracted out. "Satisfaction guaranteed is my motto," he said brightly.

Midnight found them at the site Terry had given them, alongside a cutoff on the road leading to Korat. Their transport, an ancient C-47, was in a grove of banana palms. "God, won't those things ever quit flying?" Rossen whispered.

The pilot, a skin-and-bones-thin Aussie wearing a Dodgers' baseball cap, was waiting for them. In the lights of their van he looked cadaverous, thin as a wet dream. Blond lank hair hung to his shoulders. He was wearing a tissue-thin, once-blue denim shirt washed to a near white, old jeans, and cowboy boots; a 9-mm Walther P-38 in the original German holster completed his ensemble.

They pulled the van over and parked it in the grove of banana palms, where it'd be out of sight. The pilot sauntered over and introduced himself. "Aye, mates. I'm Jack. Aussie Jack. Wonder why they call me that." He laughed, showing large yellow teeth and a definite need for a visit to a prominent orthodontist.

Tommy growled at him. "Yeah, I think we can figure that out. Now, get over here and give us a hand with this gear."

Aussie Jack did as he was told. After all, this little trip was twenty thou Yankee to him. Not bad for an evening's outing, even if he did have to kick back five to Terry, the bloody bandit.

Everything Jones had laid on for them was neatly packed in boxes. They had gone through it earlier. Jones had done them righteous. All they had asked for and a few other things as well. Two Model 1911 .45s which had been customized. Suppressors for the weapons, cammies, face paint, webbing, canteens, survival kits for the webbed belts. And the armored vests.

As Tommy and Aussie Jack loaded up, Rossen took the rifles and pistols aside, set an 8 by 10 piece of white paper at fifty meters, and went back to his rifle. Loaded, checked the action, mounted the Starlight, and took sight on the hand-drawn bull and fired three rounds. Checking his mark, he was satisfied. He knew how it was shooting. One click up and it was ranged for three hundred meters. Anything under or over that he could adjust for with Kentucky windage. Tommy then came over and did the same thing. Three rounds and he was zeroed. The pistols weren't bad. You just had to know where they were putting them, then you could compensate if you didn't have time to fine-tune them to your own specs.

Satisfied, they loaded up in the old bird, wondering how many missions she had flown in the last thirty-five or forty years.

Jack lifted off with a clear silver moon to guide him through the night, and took up a compass heading which would take him over Chiang Mai where he'd turn toward the Burma border. He knew the area well. There were several landmarks that he'd be able to use and he knew of at least three different dirt strips he'd be able to set down on with no problem, the farthest of them six clicks from the camp, the nearest only two. He told this to Rossen, who said to take the far one if he could. Less chance of someone on the deck hearing them come in.

"Righto, me buckos. You have it. Let me see now: We have about two hours flight time. It's not far at all in good weather like this. So just lean back and enjoy the ride while old Aussie Jack mothers you and this wonderful piece of design engineering to your appointed destination."

Rossen snarled at him. "Jack, shut the fuck up and fly." He did.

During the flight, they changed into the outfits Jones had provided for them, putting the armored vests on last. They knew things were going rapidly, but if they didn't move they'd probably lose the targets. Not that Rossen really gave a damn at this point. If he didn't get them this year, next year would be just as good. But Tommy wanted Yoshi, and that was all there was to it. They'd go and trust to the intel, equipment, and "Smith."

Five minutes from their landing zone, Jack yelled back for them to find a place to sit. The landing gear went down, and Jack came in skimming the tops of the trees. A bump, a cutback on the engines, and they trundled bumpily to a halt. Whatever the Aussie was, he knew how to deal with the old bird.

They didn't wait for him to taxi to the far end and turn around. He could do that after they were gone.

Taking his gear and slinging it on his back, Rossen said, "It's 0221. If we're not back by 0830, then go on without us. Got that?"

"Right, guv. Clear as rain."

They pulled out, heading into the trees on the north side of the dirt strip. Rossen took a compass reading, lined it up, and pointed. Tommy took the lead. He moved the best and had an instinct for direction once he was given a heading. He wouldn't need to stop as often as Rossen to find out their course. Which wouldn't be too difficult anyway: They would hit a valley, follow it to the end, and move to the right. There, about one click away, was the lumber camp. Just to the north of it was the compound they wanted.

Rossen ran over everything Jones had given them, the faces, the terrain, and the information about the possibility of there being a setup. If there was, it would change the approach a bit.

Once they cleared the mouth of the valley they could see the lights of the lumber camp in a break in the trees; they had their beacon. Moving out in a semicircle, they went toward the compound, where Yoshi and the others were waiting for them. Neither of them had any doubts that they were expected.

When they reached a point about half a click from the compound, they took a break. There was no conversation; they knew what they had to do. Each would take a different direction and scope out the area with the starlight scopes on the rifles. There was nothing more for them to do except do it.

If there were going to be any surprises there would be someone outside the camp trying to catch them between the house or the perimeter guards when they made their move. Put yourself into the mind of your enemy and think like him and you were usually not too far off. It helped keep you breathing a while longer also.

Tommy found his man first. The Russian KGB might be fine for urban work, but this guy didn't know shit about the jungle. His position —from where he could watch the back of the house—was an obvious one. The foliage he had piled up to lie behind didn't match what grew around him, and he moved a lot. Tommy could almost hear him breathing even at a distance. Adjusting the scope, he moved it till he found the face, peering out of the dark through a break in the bushes.

The Russian's face glowed in the green haze of the scope. Tommy couldn't let him make any sounds, so the shot would have to be a head one. Settling down, he set the reticle to where it intersected on the bridge of the man's nose.

From forty feet, there was no way he could miss. Taking his breath in, he let his body mold to the earth. The rifle settled and the trigger slack was taken up. He fired twice. The suppressor didn't completely kill sound, but it distributed it and made it harder to hear and identify. From a hundred or so meters one would hear little if anything, and then it would be indistinct. It could have been no more than a big bird farting.

The back of the Russian's head separated. Only his legs trembling in death spasm made any movement. He was brain dead. That's one.

Jones had said there were at least two. Tommy moved on, making his way around to the front where he could see the face of the house behind a tall apron of razor-edged wire. He found Rossen sitting, waiting for him.

"Okay, Tommy, let's go get them. This side's secure."

The guards on the wire came next. They were patrolling in pairs. Two quick shots each and they ceased to exist. One made a *shushing* sound as air escaped from a ruptured lung.

They moved to the wire, Tommy laying back and covering Rossen as he examined it. It wasn't electric, just plain everyday wire. Taking out his cutters, Rossen snipped a hole in the fence, using one hand to keep the wire from snapping back on him. He cut close to each tie on the wire. In two minutes they had a way in.

Rossen crossed first, lay down, took up a position, and covered Tommy as he came through. They were inside, and inside was where they wanted to be. All that was left was the house. Lights came from inside. They could hear talking, and someone singing softly. It wasn't Thai. They were there. A few more minutes and this would all be over.

Yoshi knew they were there. He couldn't have explained how, but he knew. The same feelings he had had in his dream were back. Whatever it was, was out there. He moved to where he would be out of line with the windows and doors. There was a circuit breaker on the wall nearest him.

The others saw him move. They didn't feel or sense anything, but there was something about the way the Japanese moved which said: *Watch me if you wish to live.* And the Russian had told them they might have company. They tightened up on their weapons. Ready.

Cherny stood by, an AK-47 in his hand. He was in the rear bedroom watching them. He had heard nothing, but the way the others were moving their bodies said something was going to happen. Good! Soon he would have what he wanted. He still wondered how Yoshi was going to react when he saw his cousin coming to kill him. He had not told him of that, wanting it to be a surprise.

The door exploded inward. A half pound of

C4 blew it apart, stunning everyone in the room except Yoshi. He had felt something. In a rush, he had thrown his body back into the bedroom, kicking Cherny down as he rolled to the side, opened his mouth, and covered his ears. Cherny stared at him as if he'd gone mad. The world exploded. And the killing began. Tommy and Rossen rushed in to catch the enemy while they were still stunned.

Tommy shot Hasan as he was trying to struggle to his knees, his automatic rifle held slack in one hand as if he didn't have the strength to bring it to his shoulder . . . which he did not. Brains joined the dust floating in the air. Rossen took out Yousef with two quick bursts of three, tearing the man's back out as he scrambled along the floor trying to make it to the bedroom. The others just lay where they were, dazed, blood and serous fluid coming from ears, noses, and mouths, from things that had ruptured inside them.

A thud turned the Americans' heads around. A grenade had hit the floor between the two terrorists. Tommy threw Rossen back out the doorway, where he reeled on his heels then hit deck. The grenade exploded with a dull thump. Tommy couldn't move. His arms and legs didn't belong to him anymore. They were far away, distant, his mind couldn't reach them.

Rossen came up to his knees in time to be kicked in the face by Cherny, who had rushed out as soon as the grenade went off. He passed over Tommy thinking him to be as dead as the two Palestinians. Blood trailed down his face where a splinter from the door had torn a gash in his scalp.

He was exultant. "I have you, you son of a bitch!" he yelled at Rossen in Russian. "I have you." The bore of the AK came down. Rossen could see the whitening of the trigger finger and knuckles as he took up the slack. Then Cherny's normally well groomed head exploded. His right eye became a black, gory cavern as the back of his skull opened up to permit the exit of his source of intelligence which had changed its form into one more closely resembling a large clot of black grape jelly.

His legs collapsed and Cherny fell over Rossen, who tried to push him off. A voice yelled from the trees, "I promised Green I'd look after you." Then it was gone. Jones had at last gotten into the game.

Rossen tried to get up but just didn't have the strength. He knew he wasn't badly hurt, it was just a concussion, but he couldn't function. And Tommy. What about Tommy? Was he alive? Did the grenade get him?

Tommy felt a hand touch him. Trying to focus his eyes, he heard a soft voice say to him in Japanese, "So it was you, cousin. I am glad.

But this is not how it should end. Come to me. Remember our youth and you will know where to find me. But let it be just you and me as when we were children.

"Come to me, cousin, and remember, I love you."

TWENTY-THREE

AH, IT WAS GOOD TO SIT BESIDE THE HOT SPRINGS OF one's youth. To open the senses to the vapors which rose from the boiling heart of the earth. Clear, crystal skies. Carefully tended gardens, sculptured and cared for over five hundred years. Here was peace, continuity, the grace of the ancients. To touch gently the blossom of a chrysanthemum, delicately so as not to bruise the petals, only enough to be able to sense the flower, not take it.

Yoshi knew he was coming. There was no other place for him to go. It would all end here. The place where they had played as children. He had always won their encounters between the honored samurai, the part he always took, and the treacherous and dastardly *ronin*. He always won. Or did his cousin permit him to win because he knew the winning was more important for him? A good thought. A kind thought.

A blue and gold butterfly rested, gently waving gossamer wings in the delicate wafting breeze which softly moved the petals of the flowers, and slid over the sun-faded reeds and deep green grass surrounding the ponds. Yoshi knew that if he had wished he could have reached out and touched the delicate wings with a finger and not have disturbed the creature or marred its beauty.

He had prepared himself carefully for the day, not wishing by carelessness to do less than honor. His hair was freshly cut, the front part shaved back to a line even with his sideburns. He wished his hair had been long enough to form a classic samurai topknot, but it was not. His robes were of gray silk, decorated with concentric circles of black thread mixed with gold. It was worn over a loose, pure white cotton tunic. An obi of burgundy red was cinched around his waist. Not too tight, only firm enough to keep the folds of his *hakata* in proper place.

Across his lap, resting in its sheath of sandalwood, ebony and sharkskin, was his katana. My father's sword and mine, he thought. At his waist he wore the companion blade, the shorter weapon called *tanto*, which, with the katana, made the *dai-sho*, the double swords of the samurai. Perhaps he was just a foolish romantic who wished to live impossible dreams. If so, he would not exchange his fantasy for the reality of others. The fantasy was his and much richer, more true, than the dirt-bound philosophy of merchants and eaters of carrion.

He tried to float away into the meditation rites of *zazen*, keeping his mind clear of all except the butterfly. He tried to reach out and enter the soon-to-die creature. To feel what it felt as the soft rays of Ameratsu's holy light filtered through the blue and gold wings. He almost reached it.

"I am glad you came, cousin." He didn't turn. There was no need to fear an attack from the rear, a coward's act. "I have often thought of you, and looked forward to this day since first I learned you were the one. Is it not perfect for such an occasion? Beauty and death should always greet each other as friends." Turning the upper part of his body, he looked up, smiling. "I hear they call you Tommy. Such an American thing, these silly names. But that is of no import if it pleases you."

Yoshi looked around the garden. It was empty but for the two of them. "It is well that you came alone. What must be done in this place of memories and love is not for outsiders. Though I admit I do have respect for the abilities of your American associate, he would not appreciate my intentions."

Tommy moved over, kneeling down to sit

where he could see Yoshi's face. For the first time he spoke. "He is not my associate. He is my friend. We have been through many battles together and he has never failed me."

Yoshi bowed his head in acknowledgment of the rebuke. "Forgive me, cousin. I have no right to be disrespectful of your friend. It was a bad choice of words. I apologize."

Tommy bowed his head slightly, accepting the statement as fact. Yoshi never lied. If he said something, he meant it. He was truly sorry for his words. "I understand, Yoshi-san." He looked around the playground of his youth. He, too, recalled those days when they played at this place among the flowers and ponds.

Yoshi's dress and hair did not surprise him. Neither did the *dai-sho*. "Is there no other way, Yoshi-san?" He moved his hooked hand and frightened the butterfly from its flowery perch to drift with the breeze until it was lost from sight. Both sets of eyes followed its unsteady flight.

Yoshi had heard of Tommy's lost hand, but not of how it had come to pass.

"Ah, I shall call you Tommy now, for you have gone away from us. No, there is no other way. I shall not go to a court ruled by lesser beings and be judged by men with no honor. But see that I have been thoughtful and prepared all that is necessary for this day."

He pointed with the sheathed katana over

Tommy's shoulder. Resting on a moss-covered boulder by the edge of one of the steaming ponds was a katana and a *tanto*. Beside them, near the edge of the water, nestled in green lush grass, was a wicker basket similar to the kind taken on picnics.

Yoshi smiled, pleased at Tommy's calm acceptance of the scenario. "In the basket I have rice cakes and tea. We shall eat and drink. Then when the basket is empty, we shall do what has to be done. And one of us will fill the basket with the other's head. It shall be our *kubi oki*, our head bucket."

A flight of white herons passed overhead, going to their nests in the marshes on the other side of the mountains. Yoshi's eyes followed them. They were truly free of earthly bonds. "Will you set me free this day, cousin? Or shall it be you who soars unfettered from this existence, to join all those who have passed before?"

Gracefully, he rose to his feet. No move was threatening. There was no need for threats this day. All would be done in its time. With smooth, nearly dancelike steps Yoshi moved to the moss-covered boulder. Carefully, he set the katana and its companion blade where they would rest secure against the bole of a willow tree. Then he brought the basket over, resuming his place in front of Tommy.

Removing two delicate cups and a pot

wrapped in cloth to keep the aromatic brew warm, he asked, "Shall I pour, or would you rather?"

"No, I think you should continue to be the host."

With the style of a geisha performing the tea ceremony, Yoshi poured for them, offering Tommy the thin-shelled cup with both hands, holding it only by the tips of his fingers. Bowing his head, he presented the *cha* to his cousin, who accepted it with his one good hand. After pouring his own and sucking in the hot brew with a strong intake of breath, which brought just the right amount of air in to provide contrast to the palate between hot and cold, he nodded, indicating Tommy's amputated limb.

"Will you tell me of it?"

Tommy saw no reason not to. He didn't want to rush the day. This would be the last time they would ever sit and talk as friends and companions.

"It is a good tale. To put it simply, I was taken prisoner by a North Vietnamese sniper . . ."

Yoshi clicked his teeth in disapproval. To be taken prisoner was not a good thing. One lost much karma.

Tommy knew this and continued after tasting his own tea. "I was knocked unconscious and when I came to, this sniper had decided to use me to draw out my partner, Rossen. He cut my hand from me and sent it to Rossen to let him know of my fate if he should refuse to come and meet him. Then he gave him the place and the time and Rossen came. The rest is obvious. If Rossen would have died, then I would have too, and should not be here with you at this moment."

Nodding his head, Yoshi said, "Ah, that is better. You had no opportunity to kill yourself before being taken. And it is also good that your friend came for you and saved you for this day. I would have it no other way. This is the best way for all."

Setting his cup down, he offered rice cakes, which Tommy politely declined, claiming to have eaten well earlier.

"Then, cousin, I must ask you if your hand, or the lack of it, troubles you. It was thoughtless of me to place two blades for you here. I was not thinking. Please forgive my carelessness. If your missing hand does incapacitate you, and there were sufficient time for me to regain my strength, I would cut my own hand off."

Tommy had no doubt that Yoshi would have done exactly as he said. Shaking his head from side to side, he replied pleasantly, "It does not much hinder me. I have learned to use it in different ways. And they do say that when one loses part of the body, the rest grows stronger."

From his pocket he removed a long white sack, something like a tobacco pouch. He took out a blade with the curved chisel tip of a *nambam-bo*, removed his hook, and screwed the blade in place as he laughed. "At least now I can never drop my knife, even by accident."

Yoshi grinned widely for the first time. "Ah, *so desu ka!* Yes, most interesting. That is good. But to make everything proper so there is no disadvantage, how should we do it? Would it be best for me to bind my left arm behind me or to forgo the companion blade altogether? Tell me, cousin. Which do you think would be best?"

Tommy replied slowly, "The companion is rarely used, but I have developed some skill in two-blade play. With your two hands on the hilt of the katana you will be much stronger but I think my attachment will make all even. If that is acceptable to you."

Yoshi hissed between his teeth, a sign of pleasure. "It is most acceptable, cousin. And, I think, a fair decision for all. Now, if you are ready, perhaps we should continue with steel in our hands. I would not have us lose this day's beautiful light and color."

Tommy smiled gently. "As you wish, Yoshi. But tell me one thing before we play our last game of samurai and *ronin*, for there will never be another opportunity to ask and I would have this final favor from you."

"This day I will tell you anything you wish, cousin. You have but to ask. For as you said, I am your host this day."

Leaning slightly forward, his shadow moving over the teacup, Tommy said, "Why have you done these things? I know that you are not political. All your life you have despised politicians and their philosophies."

Yoshi laughed agreeably, showing small, even white teeth. "Of course I am not political, cousin. I have no use for those savages. I have more in common with an earthworm than those pariahs."

"Then why?"

"I used them for my own purpose. I believe it was the Englishman Shakespeare who said something to the effect that all the world is a stage and we are just players. I used them to set my stage so that I could play the role meant for me. Nothing more. I am the last samurai. The petty bickerings of slavish stooges means nothing. I had to test myself in fire to make me pure enough to be ready for this day, which I knew would come. If it were not you sitting with me, there would be another and the play would continue, though I am certain not so gracefully."

Tommy bowed his head at the compliment, accepting it as truth.

Yoshi continued, his small, incredibly strong fingers stroking the fine sharkskin covering of his sword sheath. "You see, I have to die. But it must be done properly, with style and grace. I have to pit myself against the best this world has to offer. I have need to challenge myself. To reach out for my limits and face the infinite with a clear mind and calm heart. This could not be done any other way at this time. I reject life; therefore, I have no fear of death. Which does not mean I shall make its coming easy. My life must be taken from me. I will not give it up easily. To do that would be a failure. Therefore, cousin, you are now here to do that very thing. If you can."

He placed his hands out, open in a gesture reminiscent of a plea. "If you are ready, come, let us dance with good steel and read the final lines to this play of ours."

TWENTY-FOUR

TAKING HIS SHIRT OFF, TOMMY, WITH REGRET AT contaminating the springs, used it to wash the blood from his body. Then he tore the shirt into strips and made a crude bandage which he wrapped around his chest. Over this, he zipped up his windbreaker almost to the neck to conceal the injury from questioning eyes.

The swords and their companion blades he threw as far as he could out into the steaming waters. It was best if everything that could be was left behind, here in this place of quiet, now untroubled, dreams.

He took with him only the basket.

He was very tired by the time he returned to the inn where Rossen waited anxiously. He'd gone through his second pack of smokes as his mind played out one horrible fantasy after another. He promised himself that if Tommy was killed, he'd go after Yoshi till hell froze over, and teach that son of a bitch something about true dedication. Maybe not in the way that he and Tommy understood, but in the way that hate and vengeance could drive one to forget all other things in life.

Tommy had not gone through the lobby; instead, he took a path to the side of the office and restaurant where Rossen's bungalow was set at the edge of a small grove of pines. He had to drag up enough saliva to give a thin whistle to let Rossen know he was coming in.

Rossen was at the door before the soft sound was completed. He had waited in the room, afraid to be in public, not wanting to take the chance that anything could occur which would set him off. He'd promised Tommy to do nothing. He had done just that. Nothing except worry.

When he let Tommy in, he knew he was hurt. The pain around the eyes was evident. In his one good hand was a picnic basket. It looked heavy.

Tommy nodded at him as he half stumbled into the room, setting the basket down at the side of his bed.

He wanted to sleep. But there was no time. They had to be gone before Yoshi's body, or what was left of it, was discovered. It wasn't likely that it would be found very soon, but you never knew, and they could not answer any questions.

"It's time to go, Jim. It's over. At least it's

over for here, but there is still one more thing I have to do before I can feel that everything has been laid to rest.''

His eyes went to the basket. In a rush, as blood drained from his face, Rossen knew what was inside the innocent straw.

"Okay, Tommy, you get ready and I'll make the call."

Tommy had no objections. It was best if Rossen called it in.

Tommy went to wash himself and change into a clean shirt after he dressed his cut. It wasn't bad, merely somewhat painful, but he'd had worse.

The familiar voice came on the line. "Do you have anything to report?"

Rossen would have liked to bust Jones in the mouth. Instead, he said only, "It's over. The last has gone south. But we'll need a clean-up crew here."

He gave him the location of the springs.

"We'd appreciate it if you could expedite this. As for us, we're going home. Don't call us. We'll call you."

Something he planned never to do.

Jones hung up the phone, placing it with great care back on the cradle. He wished he'd had someone there to tell it to. All he could do was smile to himself. They had done it. The last of the terrorists had gone down. Goddamn it! If only there was some way to let the world know the real story. Maybe it might make some people on both sides think twice. But they had done it. Goddamn, it was good.

He wanted to call Green and Manchester, but decided to wait until he got back to the States, where he'd have a more secure line. Overseas calls were too easy to tap into, and he didn't want to pass this on in half-silly phrases. He wanted the pleasure of telling them, plain and simple, how it had been done and what they had bought for their money. It was going to be a pleasure.

Before they went back to Tokyo they made one small side trip, turning off onto a narrow dirt road which ran between green paddy fields until it turned off into a rocky cleft which led into some hills. There, at the edge of a small canyon, was an ancient gray building carved out of the native stone. At the pine-and-cedar-lined walkway leading to it was a large torii, with ancient ropes dangling from the cornices.

The building was two stories and very plain. Only a man-sized brass bell, which had turned gray-green with age, decorated the outside. It was hung from the branches of a living tree. To the side was a large log suspended on ropes from what looked like a large sawhorse. Rossen knew that temple priests would on occasion strike the huge bell with the log. He wondered what it would sound like in this valley where sounds would echo from the rocky walls of the gorge.

Tommy left him in the rental car and went inside, carrying the basket. He wasn't gone long, ten or twelve minutes, and returned without his burden. He seemed to be more relaxed and fell asleep within minutes after they had turned around to make the drive back to Shuzinji and the train to Tokyo.

In Tokyo they'd found a doctor who did not suffer from overweening curiosity and who stitched up Tommy's chest for a fee ten times normal. It still ached, and would for some time to come, but that wasn't what bothered Rossen as he accepted a cup of coffee from the smiling JAL stewardess.

Tommy made a few small sounds in his sleep. He was dreaming. Rossen had several times been tempted to ask him what had taken place by the springs. He didn't. Everyone was entitled to some things meant for them alone. If Tommy wanted to tell him one day, he would.

Tommy slept restlessly. There were images, but none strong enough to dominate his sleep, only trouble him by their wavering presence at the edge of the dark.

He had done all he could. The head of Yoshi had been taken to a priest of the Shinto they had known as children. He would perform all the proper rites and see that the ashes which remained when Yoshi was consumed by the flames were laid to rest and prayed over in the family plot.

Now he was the last of his line. The last Tomanaga. But had he buried the last samurai?

His dreams became clearer. The last moments by the springs were replayed. Once more he bent to look into the eyes of Yoshi as his cousin's lips moved. The smiling face of Yoshi changed. He was looking at his own face. The lips moved again, whispers of air brushed past the paling lips, lips which smiled at him, saying, "When all is done, there is left only . . . SEPPUKU."